"An exciting mix of conspiracy, murder and mayhem . . . Commander George Gideon of Scotland Yard, the standout creation of J. J. Marric, performs his usual stalwart service for queen and country."
—*Buffalo News*

"Commander Gideon is the cream of the detective crop . . . a creation as distinct and separate from all others as is Nero Wolfe or Maigret or Sherlock Holmes . . . a policeman all too human but with a stroke of genius."   —*Fort Worth Star-Telegram*

"A real delight . . . one of Gideon's best . . . engrossing, credible, exciting, full of emotion and crammed with intrigue . . . highly entertaining . . . as an introduction to the Scotland Yard detective, this one can't be topped."   —*Amarillo News*

Watch for these other exciting J. J. Marric mysteries
published by Popular Library:

GIDEON'S FOG

J.J.MARRIC
GIDEON'S PRESS

POPULAR LIBRARY • NEW YORK

POPULAR LIBRARY EDITION
December, 1976

Copyright © 1973 by J. J. Marric

Library of Congress Catalog Card Number: 73-4154

Published by arrangement with Harper & Row, Publishers, Inc.

ISBN: 0-445-00426-6

Editor's Note

John Creasey, with whom I worked happily for many years, died early in June, while this book was being printed.

Harper's published him under his own name originally, then both as John Creasey and as J. J. Marric, and for many years we published him only as Marric, the creator of our friend Commander Gideon of Scotland Yard.

I am hopeful that John, who was farsighted and prolific, has left another Gideon manuscript somewhere in Salisbury, so that, though, alas, we won't be seeing John himself again, Gideon will be with us for a little longer.

We will miss John, off and on paper, very much indeed.

JOAN KAHN

1

No Delivery

GEORGE GIDEON OPENED the front door of his house in
Harrington Street, Fulham, one of hundreds of solid, red-
brick Victorian houses in that residential part of London
now in greater demand, perhaps, than ever in their exis-
tence. The brick was weathered and its deepened red was
shown more vividly by the glossy white paint at window,
door, and ledges. Even at their plainest, the Victorians
had built fussily, and the present fad of painting everything that wasn't brick in high gloss revealed just how
many ledges jutted out here and jutted out there. Kate,
Gideon's wife, had tentatively suggested—and no doubt
hoped for—a pale blue, or even pink or primrose yellow,
but Gideon had said, "Love, it's like dolling a sixty-year-
old up to look like sixteen."

Now the white had lost a little of its gloss, and showed
up with dignity against the many pastel shades nearby,
which belonged more to the Riviera, or conceivably to the
more artistic, mixed-period areas of Chelsea only a mile
or two nearer the heart of London. Gideon and Kate
were equally satisfied with the result.

Gideon, however, was not pleased that morning, because the newspapers were late. He opened the door and
looked left, the direction from which the newsboy came
on his bicycle, but saw only a few hurrying men and
fewer girls, whose heads and shoulders showed, curiously
disembodied, above the roofs of the tightly packed cars.

No cyclist was in sight.

He closed the door a shade too loudly, and went down the step along the tiled path and past the small, neat lawn and the trim privet hedge, gave a last look left and then swung to the right. He was a big man with thick shoulders and a short neck who gave an impression of restrained power, shoulders bearing slightly forward and hinting at determination to get to wherever he was going as soon as he possibly could. At the corner he turned right, casting a single glaring glance behind him along the now empty street.

"Lazy little beggars," he grumbled. "No one wants to get up in the morning these days."

He strode on to the garage and unlocked it, then laughed at himself. His whole mood changed. He knew that it would swing back to exasperation soon, although probably not so far. He pushed the overhead door of the garage up and it ran smoothly; oil that he had put on the runners during the weekend had now spread over squeaking patches. He got into his own roomy Rover, not a police car, reversed out, parked, closed the door, and locked it. His mood was at least partly because he was home alone for a few days. Kate had gone to stay with their oldest married daughter, Prudence, for a change of scene. Gideon had urged her to go, had virtually pushed her out of the house, but he hadn't bargained for Penny —their youngest daughter, and still single—going to Scotland at the same time, for a piano recital with the B.B.C. Symphony Orchestra because the pianist from Poland who had been billed couldn't appear. For Penelope it was a chance in a thousand; for Gideon it meant getting his own morning tea, breakfast, and even supper. Of course, he could have waited until he reached Scotland Yard and breakfasted in the canteen, but on a bad traffic morning the journey could take forty minutes, and he had been hungry on waking. He grinned as he thought of it; he'd had to get his own supper last night and hadn't had more than a couple of small chops and some grilled tomatoes.

He was ready to drive off. Just in case the paper boy was coming, he drove along his route, although there was a shorter way to the main road, but the only cyclist was a schoolboy with a fishing rod fastened across his back and a canvas bag dangling from his saddle. That was probably what the regular boy was doing—playing truant from his job! It was remarkable how one came to take certain facilities for granted: the morning newspaper, the post, the milk, a dozen and one things; it was astonishing how resentful one became if a service which was maintained for two hundred consecutive days, say, failed on the two hundred and first.

At least he hadn't been put out this morning simply because the routine had broken down; it wasn't just pique. He had come in late the previous night, after the news on television, and thus had missed the latest word on the threatened dock strike. All the radio had said was that there would be another meeting that afternoon, and he wanted to be briefed when he reached the office because there was to be a meeting of commanders and their deputies to make plans in case the emergency did come about.

He made a series of turns and came out into New Kings Road, turned right, and pulled up outside the newspaper shop from which his newsboy came. He waited for a stream of small cars to pass and then opened his door, and went into the small shop, one window of which was filled with large glass jars of sweets, the other with equally colorful paperback books; a few years ago half the covers on them would have been considered pornographic. Inside the shop, one counter displayed sweets and cigarettes, the other toys and books, magazines and newspapers; but there was none of today's papers. A gray-haired man came from an open doorway at the back as Gideon entered; a bell must ring or a light show whenever one entered the shop.

"Good morning, sir." The man looked at him as if he were puzzled.

"Good morning. My newspapers—"

"Oh. I'm sorry about any inconvenience, sir," the man interrupted; he uttered the words in parrotlike fashion. "It's the strike, none of the Allied group's papers came out this morning—not in the London area, anyway. Aren't you Mr. Gideon?"

"Yes."

"Well I *am* sorry, sir. You've been a customer here so long you should have had something. It's the boys these days, they never *think*." He put a hand beneath the counter. "There's a *Times,* sir, or a *Guardian.* I've popped a few under the counter for regulars, you see."

"Then I'll have the *Times,*" Gideon decided, checking an impulse to say both. The newspaper was flourished with the air of a magician, and the major headline read: DOCKS NEAR SHUTDOWN.

The man was saying something, and Gideon, reading the first sentences of the article, asked, "What was that?"

"Would you like anything else, sir—to make up for the difference in the cost of your usual three? You've seven pence to come, and it's such a nuisance changing the entries in the delivery book."

"I'll have some Players," Gideon said, remembering that he was out of cigarettes at the office. Although he did not smoke cigarettes himself, he kept a supply for visitors. As he handed over a fifty-pence piece he reflected that this man with his faintly whining voice was no fool; he looked after his regulars and slipped in a little extra business when the chance offered.

"Thank you, sir."

"Thank you." Gideon went out as two women turned in to the shop doorway. He crossed to his car and stood beside it, reading about the docks trouble. If this story could be taken at its face value, the Dock Workers' Union leaders, the Dock Employers' Federation representative, and the Minister of Production and Employment had talked until the early hours and broken up without making any progress. So things really looked bad. He rounded the car and got in. As he closed the door a policeman appeared on the other side, tapping, helmet thrusting forward, face oddly foreshortened. I must have parked where I shouldn't, Gideon thought, and schooled himself to be mild-mannered as he leaned over and wound the window down.

"Hallo," he said.

"Excuse me, sir, aren't you Mr.—*Commander*—Gideon?"

"Yes," Gideon answered shortly.

"There's a call for you, sir," the policeman told him, and with a voice tensed with pride he went on, "I thought I recognized you go in—I was just along the road, sir."

"Very observant of you." The man actually blushed. "Wait for a moment in case I need you." He flicked on his walkie-talkie contact with the Yard, slightly annoyed that he had forgotten, in his preoccupation, to switch it on earlier. One of the reasons for having his own car and not relying always on police transport was that in an official car he felt an obligation to have his receiver on all the time. They still hadn't overcome the problem of atmospherics. *Squack, squawk, eek,* it went as he said, "Commander Gideon calling Information. Over."

"Information here, sir," a man answered promptly. "There's a message from the Commissioner City Police, could you possibly go straight to his office instead of coming here."

"Yes," Gideon said.

"Thank you. I'll send word, sir."

Gideon grunted, looked up into the face of the eager police constable, and said, "I shan't need you, but thanks." He took a mental note of the number on the man's collar; went further and noted it on a pad before he drove off. This was almost a reflex action, and explained why he probably knew more men on the Metropolitan Police Force than any other individual. He waited for a break in the steady stream of traffic and moved out into the road, wondering why the City Commissioner had sent that most unusual message. The constable waved him on. Guessing motives wasn't profitable, but Gideon liked to be at least partly prepared for any situation.

Sir Giles Rook, recently appointed to his post as chief of the City Police, had held a similar position in one of the smaller African colonies before its independence and for some years afterward had been employed at the Home Office, the government Ministry which virtually controlled the nation's police forces. Rook had been the chairman of a committee which had studied the conditions of police work and the provincial forces in particular and which had recommended a number of unspectacular but quietly effective measures, mostly to do with the integration of the independent police forces, communications between them, and welfare. While several of the old-timers at City had no doubt been disappointed when he had been brought in, probably his appointment had proved one of the most popular for a long time.

Gideon had served on his committee for years. He had never come to know Rook as a human being but greatly respected him as a chairman and an administrator. There was another thing: it had become obvious that Rook had studied police forces throughout the world, was familiar with the methods of many in small, little-known countries, and was one of the few men who could reel off the multiplicity of police forces in Italy, say, or the Argentine and Japan. In one way, it was strange that he should end his career in the City of London, one of the smallest police forces and quite distinct from the Metropolitan Police Force, but in other ways it was fitting. For in the Port of London there was perhaps more direct contact with the rest of the world than any other place, not excluding Scotland Yard. While City did not control the Port of London, which had its own police force, they worked very closely together.

Gideon turned along several streets until eventually he

came to the Embankment. The sun was out, the river looked beautiful; even the comparatively undeveloped South Bank had a touch of the picturesque, with the four great stacks of the Battersea Power Station emitting only a haze of smoke. The bridges were busy and three big lorries exuding diesel fumes, which had an abominable stench, exasperated Gideon for a few minutes, until two turned off at Battersea Bridge and one in to Oakley Street. Gideon was able to go a little faster, past the old red-brick building of Scotland Yard, and really enjoy the sweep toward and beyond the new Waterloo Bridge and the Temple and the panorama of the City of London. He went through the underpass remembering how difficult and thick traffic was before the new road had been made. He reached Old Jewry, where the City Police were housed, and found two constables, with their tall helmets and gilt buttons, waiting by a parking space. One of them came forward.

"Good morning, Commander."

"Good morning."

"If you care to leave your car here, sir . . ."

"Thanks." Gideon pocketed the key, and got out.

The City Headquarters, being so much smaller, was easier to control than the Yard. Though it was in the heart of the business section of London, with the major banks and insurance companies and big commercial enterprises crowding in upon it, it had a kind of homeliness; it seemed more like one of the older Divisional Stations, although few of the men who worked there would have liked that said. One of the policemen led him, without a word, up narrow stone stairs and to the partly open door of the Commissioner's office. Rook was talking to someone when the policeman tapped on the door.

"Who is it?" Rook called.

"Commander Gideon is here, sir."

"Oh. Good!" There was a movement as of a chair, the door opened, and Rook appeared: a stocky, broad-shouldered, short-haired block of a man with an exceptionally long face and long jaw. "Thank you for coming so quickly, Commander." He shook hands and turned toward the office. "You know Inspector Lawless, don't you?"

Gideon did indeed. Lawless was one of the chiefs of the Port of London Authority Police. He had once been a Yard man, a sergeant, and had worked with Gideon when Gideon had been a Chief Inspector. He checked an impulse to exclaim, "Percy, you've put on weight!" and shook hands. Lawless was enormous about the middle and had three chins. Yet his face had a childlike look and his thin hair was as golden as a cherub's.

"Hallo, Percy."

"Good to see you, George."

The policeman closed the door, and Rook sat at his large, flat-topped desk. His office was sparsely furnished but spick-and-span. It overlooked an old Victorian bank building with a red-tiled roof. On either corner of the front of his desk was a large armchair, ample for both massive Gideon and fat Lawless. They sat down.

"Cigarettes?" Rook pushed a cedar box across the desk.

"No, thanks," Lawless said.

"Not for me."

"That makes three of us," said Rook, with obvious satisfaction. "George, the trouble at the docks looks like it's getting really serious, and I don't simply mean the strike itself. But Percy has heard strong rumors—"

"More than rumors," interjected Lawless. "Unofficial inside information."

"—that what is believed to be an extreme right-wing group is planning to break up the dock-gate meetings," Rook went on. "And he has heard talk that one or two extreme left-wingers have infiltrated the right-wing group and are aware of what is being planned. It has all the makings of a very nasty clash indeed. Here in the City, and out at the East India and Millwall docks for certain—possibly at all of them. If we do have serious clashes here, then they are likely to spread through the country, and it could lead to the worst trouble we've had in the docks for many years." Rook spread his hands over the desk in a quick, characteristic way. "And you don't need telling what that means in terms of the economy, industrial unrest generally, and long-term damage to the docks themselves."

Gideon listened to all this with sinking heart.

This was a period when one lived on a precipice of labor troubles and economic disaster; one had for years. It was as if Britain had created a society in which the only way to get justice for one group was to create injustice and hardship for others. Some believed this to be a perpetual problem, others believed that the ever-shortening periods of industrial peace developed a strength which would eventually overcome the causes of conflict. He wasn't one who thought so. Not a politician, and as dispassionate as a man could be, he felt a deepening ache at the wounding of his country and its people, and was only too aware that the consequences of this wounding injured many others in the world. But he was, above all, a policeman. His position made him stand apart from the causes of the disputes, whether they were basic or short-term causes. Only now and again, when something like this trouble threatened, was there anything he could even try to do. In keeping the peace, as it was called, one could cause bitter enmity. If open conflict resulted, the police would automatically become involved but they would be regarded as ciphers: charges of brutality would be bandied about; the television screens and the newspapers would be full of pictures of clashes not between the opposing groups but between the police and one group or the other.

Before he could say what he felt, though, there was one question he had to ask, and even that question caused a problem because it might look as if he were trying to evade responsibility.

Both men were watching him as he made himself ask, "Why send for me, sir? Why not Uniform? Or the Commissioner? Isn't it more their province than mine?"

2

Unofficial

To GIDEON's enormous relief, Rook began to smile and Lawless gave a broad grin. Whatever these reactions implied, it was not that they believed him to be evading the issue. Both men began at once.

"We were saying—"

"Percy had just prepared me for—"

"What my first question would be," Gideon finished for Rook. He chuckled, feeling in better spirits than he had been all the morning. What trifling things could lift or sink a man's heart! "It's a valid question, sir."

"Yes," Rook admitted. "I'm not sure the answer is as valid, though. At the moment this is unofficial. Lawless got his tip from someone outside the Force and came straight to me because he thought I would keep it under my hat while we had time to think. And I thought you would do the same. Once this gets deep into the official channels, we don't know where it will end."

"Couldn't be more right," said Lawless emphatically.

"The problem is, where will it end if it doesn't get stopped?" asked Gideon.

"Precisely." Rook sat very erect in his chair. "We couldn't stand still and do nothing. We would have to have men on stand-by, so would Lawless and the P.L.A. everywhere, and so would you. A show of police force at a dockers' strike meeting will enrage the dockers. We'll be shot at from all sides and accused of being responsible for inciting trouble—expecially as the extreme right-wingers will almost certainly avoid a clash with us. We would in effect do their job for them without causing them any trouble." Rook paused, looking almost anxiously at Gideon, and went on: "Do you see what I'm driving at?"

"Oh, yes, sir," Gideon answered. "I see only too well."

"Don't you agree with the reasoning?"

"Provided we went in to keep the opposing factions apart, yes, but if we were simply on duty and the right-wingers didn't turn up, we'd certainly be the trouble-makers. It's almost as if someone leaked the story so as to put us on the spot, isn't it?"

"*Could* that be your informant's motive?" Rook asked Lawless, as if startled.

"I'd be bloody surprised," the fat man answered. "But I couldn't swear it isn't. Doesn't make much difference, though, does it? We know what's in the wind. If we do nothing and there's trouble, we'll know we should have tried to stop it. If we take official action— Oh, George is right," Lawless went on. "All I can say, George, is that I don't know what's best."

"George," Rook asked, in a no-nonsense tone, "what do you advise?"

In all his years of experience, Gideon had never before run into a situation anything like this: top policemen withholding knowledge from top policemen! It had a funny side and it had a deadly serious side, and now he was as deeply involved as either of them. Or if he joined them in their conspiracy of silence, he could be. Rook's readiness to ignore the rules and regulations of the "proper chan-nels" did not really surprise him; in the chair of his com-mittee he had always been inclined to cut both corners and red tape. Percy Lawless surprised Gideon very much indeed, for Lawless had always been a stickler—even overpunctilious. Perhaps there was a relaxation of disci-pline in the Port of London Authority force; or was it that he had gone as high as he could ever hope to go and was therefore less on his guard?

Gideon remarked, "You know this would be primarily a Uniform job, don't you?"

Rook nodded; Lawless made no comment. Uniform at the Yard, at this time, was undergoing a difficult period, with a young, very able, almost overefficient commander at its head, one who would carry out every job he had to do in a manner not far short of ruthless. If he heard even a breath of this in advance, he would be after the Assistant Commissioner of the Uniformed Branch to take immediate action, and that could be so easily premature.

The two men were acutely aware of these things, of course. They had sent for Gideon because they felt they could rely on him at least to sympathize with, if not share, their attitudes, and he was sitting back and snorting like a disgruntled bull. At the same time, he was letting thoughts drift through his mind. This was the kind of situation he would like to ponder, forget, and ponder again until his subconscious produced some viable new ideas.

"George," Rook said quietly, "I know how you like to chew the cud, but there isn't much time."

"Hardly any time," Lawless remarked gloomily.

"But there's a little," Gideon replied more vigorously. "Is the coffee they bring you as good as ever?"

"Better," Rook said, and lifted a telephone, speaking almost as soon as he'd put the receiver to his ear. "Send some coffee in at once," he ordered, and put the receiver down and pushed back his chair. He was now completely relaxed, all impression of tension and urgency gone. "It's good to see you," he went on. "It must be over two years since our last committee meeting."

"Three," Gideon observed.

"Is it really as long as that?"

"Must be four since you came along to see us, George," remarked Lawless. "There ought to be a way to get together sometimes without all the pomp and ceremony of the police ball and official occasions."

"I rather enjoy the big nights," Rook remarked. "But

I had to miss last year's. Touch of influenza," he added.

"*I* had to miss the previous year," Gideon said. "My wife was ill."

"Kate all right now?" inquired Lawless.

"Fine, thanks, she—" Gideon broke off because the door opened and an elderly man brought in a tray of coffee and biscuits, and also because of an expression on the fat man's face which puzzled him. Could it be pain? Not physical pain, but some kind of hurt brought on by recollection?

Rook poured, and there were the usual questions: "Sugar?" "Cream?" "How much?" until at last they were sitting back and drinking coffee, Gideon still puzzled by Lawless's expression but no longer preoccupied by it. It was good, strong coffee, served American-style with thin cream; he had acquired a taste for it on his brief visits to New York and other cities in the United States. Now, looking at Rook, he was also looking at the problem which hadn't yet gone too deep in his mind. He finished his first cup of coffee, said, "May I come again?" and as Rook took the cup, he went on in almost the same breath, "We'd better leak the information to a reliable man in Fleet Street."

"Leak?" Lawless almost squeaked.

Rook did not pause as he poured out, and did not speak.

"Yes," Gideon insisted. "We can't tell the press generally; that would have to come through official channels. Thanks." He took the proffered cup. "Of course the obvious and simplest method *is* to make it official to all the newspapers. Then both sides would expect the police to be at the dock gates in strength."

"So you haven't heard," Rook said, rather heavily.

"Heard what?"

"About the strike."

"You mean in Fleet Street?"

"Yes."

"I knew some London editions had been stopped by a

dispute," Gideon said. He didn't touch his coffee, just looked blankly at Rook, aware of a sinking feeling inside him. "How big and when?"

"The London evening papers have joined in," answered Rook. "We've just heard."

"The dailies?"

"There's a fifty-fifty chance that they'll go back to work, and it's about two-to-one against the evenings being published tonight."

"But you know how these things spread," Lawless put in.

"Yes," said Gideon gruffly. He felt more sick at heart than ever as he sipped his coffee. The lifeblood of the nation pulsed through the docks, and the minds of the people were fed mostly through the newspapers. These were the two channels, of goods and news, which were most essential to the nation. He was surprised that this blow struck so heavily. Why the hell couldn't employer and employed find a way of working together in harmony?

"These *bloody* strikes," Lawless said. It was a *cri de coeur*. "I don't know how big it is, but this group calls itself the Strike Breakers. Ever hear of them?"

"No," Gideon said.

"Strikes can be bloody, all right," agreed Rook. "The ugliest one I ever had to deal with was in M'Lawa, at the copper mines. Half the poor devils were terrified of what would happen if they downed tools, so they tried to get past the pickets. The pickets were well drilled and trained. Seven died," he went on. "At least a hundred were severely injured. I lost one man, and two were so badly wounded they had to retire. That's why——" He broke off, as if suddenly—and for him, rarely—in confusion. "Never mind."

"That's why you don't want trouble at the dock gates," Lawless observed.

"Can you think of a better reason?" asked Rook.

The reply silenced and presumably satisfied Percy Lawless, but it didn't satisfy Gideon. He placed the half-finished coffee on Rook's desk, pushed his chair back, and stood up. It was only a step or two to the window. The red-tiled house was three stories high and above a very narrow, cobbled passage, but he wasn't thinking about buildings or passages. He was telling himself that Sir Giles Rook *was* the Police Commissioner of the City of London and *was* far superior to him in rank. So there was a limit to what he should allow himself to say; certainly he shouldn't become involved in argument about motives. He had a great deal of experience to draw on, and although the situation outlined to him might be as bad as the others obviously believed, even if it were only half as bad he would still favor an unofficial approach. Any formal police action in advance of industrial conflict was always likely to be misinterpreted, and could lead to positive harm because it might undermine the faith of reasonable men in the impartiality of the police.

A couple came out of a narrow doorway, the girl slim, the youth plump; they put their arms around each other, and kissed passionately.

Gideon turned around, and said with quiet deliberation, "I think it would be better if we missed the evening newspapers, anyhow. They always give plenty of time for action to be taken. What we need is a London national morning newspaper which would squeeze the story in at the last minute. What time is the meeting, Percy?"

"Twelve noon," Lawless answered promptly.

"If a story was released by nine or ten o'clock, it would be in time," Gideon said. "I think we should try the *Daily News;* it has a special late-morning edition covering news which comes in up to about seven o'clock. If the story didn't appear, we would still have time to leak it to the B.B.C. on one of its hourly radio news broadcasts." He paused for a moment and then went on gruffly: "Mind you, a lot of our chaps would say that we should release the story to the newspapers and the B.B.C. and I.T.V. now, claiming that a proper job would be done at the docks. This way—my way—any attempt we made might go off half cocked." He looked from one to the other, suspecting that they had some reason for consulting him that they hadn't yet vouchsafed.

"George," Rook said, "if it's broadcast everywhere, then the right-wingers will know there is a spy in their ranks. If it leaks out at the last minute—well, that's the way I would prefer. But I wouldn't force the issue, although I'm convinced the information is reliable. I confess I was hoping you *would* suggest that we should let the story leak out, and a reliable Fleet Street man would be just what we want. Do you know of one? We don't."

Ah, thought Gideon. That's the crunch and that's why I'm here.

"Possibly," he said.

"One thing's certain," said Rook. "If the story is officially released by the main television news tonight, that will give us all the official time needed. By then you should know whether the morning papers are coming out. If you've a friend whom you could trust, will you talk to him?"

"We'd give you carte blanche, of course," Lawless put in eagerly. "Whichever way seemed best to you would be all right with us—with *me*. Wouldn't it be with you, Sir Giles?"

"Yes," Rook said briskly.

They were passing the buck, and in a way that was both pleasing and flattering. Gideon knew them well enough to be sure that neither would take umbrage if he decided that he should take the story to Uniform, either direct or through his deputy. He was doubling the posts of Commander and Assistant Commissioner Criminal Investigation Department for the time being, which could cause problems. The fact that Rook had sent for him showed how strongly he felt the need for discretion, but there were other factors. Rook had the strongest personal reasons for hating the very thought of trouble at the docks; he had an emotional response which could warp his judgment. And Percy Lawless also had the strongest possible reasons for not wanting trouble: a violent clash would suggest that the Port of London Authority Police could not handle their own affairs. There was little doubt that these two men had considered all this and decided that if there was a way out of their predicament, it was through him, George Gideon, because he had the ear of so many people, the entrée to so many places, and an influence that was due partly to his own reputation and personality but at least as much to the actual position itself.

"George," Lawless said, "if anyone can pull this out of the bag, you can. No one else would stand an earthly."

"I fully concur," Rook said.

"Just between you and me," said Gideon, "I think you are a pair of back-slapping, buck-passing coppers. But you might be right, all the same."

"You'll do it!" cried Rook.

"I'll try," Gideon said.

"Who—" began Lawless, happy and hopeful.

"You don't expect me to tell you who I'll try this out on, do you?" asked Gideon. "But I'll do what I can. Now if you will tell me who these right-wingers are, Percy, and all the details you can—who squealed, for instance, and how reliable the statement is . . ." He went on for a moment or two, inwardly at peace and knowing the others were, too. For the time being, the possibility of taking effective action deadened the impact of both dock strike and newspaper strike, and their potential harm.

"The right-wingers are a group we've heard rumors about for some time, an offshoot of the unionist movement dedicated to breaking strikes, hence the title the Strike Breakers. As to who gave me the story, I can't see that it would help you to know, but I've got my spies everywhere!" Lawless spread his hands. "Will that do, George?"

For the time being, Gideon knew, it had to do.

That was the very moment when Willis Murdoch, the most militant of the leaders of the dockers at the London docks, was looking across the desk—in his tiny, scrupulously tidy office, just inside the King Edward Dock Gates—at a small, red-haired old man. Murdoch was a powerful-looking, stocky man who was nearly bald, and who wore pince-nez on his broken nose. That was one of the many incongruities about the man.

"Tig," he said, "if you're making this up, I'll break you into little pieces and throw you into the river."

"But I'm not!" protested Tig, in a voice so hoarse it sounded as if every syllable hurt him. He had a look of perpetual fear on his wizened face—not without reason, for he had always fought the odds. "They're going to bring knives and clubs, I tell you, razor blades and bicycle chains, too. And I'm not the one they'll break into little pieces, either. I got just one piece of advice for you, Willy—make sure your chaps are ready to defend themselves."

"Who are these bloody Strike Breakers?" demanded Murdoch.

"I don't know who they are. I only know they're coming from all over London. I was doing a job last night and they was talking—scared the living daylights out of me, they did. I didn't need telling what they would do if they caught me. I sneaked out as soon as I could. They never knew I was there. Absolutely wasted night for me, that was."

"So you come along and try to sell me a lot of phony information for a fiver."

"It's not phony!"

"What was the name of the street?" said Murdoch.

"I tell you I don't know," protested the man called Tig. "All I know it was Highgate, in one of those long roads that lead off from the High Street. I don't know which one. I was on my bike and I'd just passed a copper, so I didn't waste any time worrying what street it was. I can tell you one thing," Tig added, with a sudden swing to dignity. "The house next door had a lovely lot of tobacco plants—night-scented stocks, don't they call them? Lovely, it was. And the place I went in was in darkness and they'd left a window open in the downstairs toilet. As soon as I got in, *they* came in."

"Did you see them?" said Murdoch.

"No, I never. I've told you I got out P.D.Q."

"All right, I'll believe you but thousands wouldn't," Murdoch said. "And those tobacco plants are called nicotiana, if you give a damn. Told anyone else about this, Tig?"

"Who the hell would I tell?"

"Just answer the question," ordered Murdoch equably.

"No one, no one at all."

"Well, keep your trap shut," said Murdoch. He took out a worn leather wallet. "Here's a couple of quid to keep the wolf from the door. If they turn up, we'll be ready for them, all right—and you'll get a fiver."

"On top o' this?" asked Tig eagerly.

"Yes."

"That's the nearest thing to money in my pocket I know." The wizened man stuffed the two pound notes into the breast pocket of his tatty tweed jacket. "I'll be seeing you, Will!" He got up and moved toward the door, grinning in a lopsided way. "But don't expect me near the docks around midday tomorrow. I wouldn't go there for all the tea in China!"

3

"Reliable Man"

GIDEON WENT into the main entrance of the *Daily News* at two-fifteen that afternoon. Behind him was a routine half-hour with his deputy, Hobbs, about a variety of cases, most of them under investigation, and none, as far as one could judge, near solution; and behind him, too, was an hour with the other commanders and their deputies, and a discussion on what steps to take if a strike really came about. There was probability, but no certainty, that the military would be called in to move foodstuffs and other perishable cargoes vital to daily living, though there would be grave trouble if that happened: clashes, or attempted clashes, between the military and the dockers, and the police—including the Criminal Investigation Department—would become deeply involved. Plans for such an emergency were always ready, of course, and under review from time to time; this morning's session was simply a refresher.

He had felt a twinge or two when Upway of Uniform, known throughout the Yard as Yew-Yew Upway, had said, with his overbearing self-confidence, "Get ready to hit anyone who threatens trouble before they start on us." Behind him also were a sandwich lunch and twenty minutes of dictation, as well as a call to Charles Mesurier, the news editor of the *Daily News*.

"Can you spare me half an hour today, Mr. Mesurier?"

"Yes, of course. What time would suit you?"

"Is two-thirty all right for you?"

"I'll make it all right," the other man had promised.

Now, waiting at a wrought-iron grille for someone to come forward from the "Enquiries" office, Gideon pondered his reasons for thinking first of Mesurier—in fact, why he had given no one else in Fleet Street a thought. He didn't know the man well, and didn't greatly like what little he knew. But of all the national press, the *News* was the paper that seemed to Gideon to present the most unslanted stories. Every newspaper had its axe to grind, its owners to satisfy, its advertisers to please, and its readers to cosset, but the *News* seemed to achieve all these things without a lot of fuss or self-advertisement. That was probably why its circulation was not far above the million mark. Despite this, however, the *Daily News* weathered every storm of strike or economic crisis, every squeeze and cutback in advertising revenue. It was privately owned by a family trust which, as far as Gideon knew, kept in the background and allowed its managers and editors to do their job unshackled, and though it suffered when the printing chapels ran into trouble with the bigger newspaper groups, it was usually the last to be shut down.

"Good afternoon, sir," a girl said from behind the grille.

"Mr. Mesurier, please. He's expecting me."

"Are you Mr. Gideon?"

"Yes," Gideon answered.

"Then if you would go up to the fourth floor, sir, someone will be waiting there to take you to Mr. Mesurier." She made the name sound like "Mesuray."

"Thank you." Gideon turned to the lifts, almost directly behind him. One attendant stood by the closed entrances to the four lift cars, all of which needed repainting and some renovation. But one opened smoothly, and when he pressed the fourth-floor button the doors closed silently and the lift rose easily; the inside of the car needed some patching and painting, too. The short journey took a long time. Gideon had a moment of apprehension that it had stopped midway between floors, but no, the doors opened with a faint whir of sound. As he stepped out, a woman in her middle forties, trim, primly dressed, with graying hair drawn tightly back from her forehead and into a bun on the nape of her neck, came along a passage which had a high wooden wall on one side and frosted-glass partitions on the other. Bells rang, typewriters clattered, footsteps tapped or thudded, a dozen people seemed to be talking at once—including the plain-looking woman.

"Mr. Gideon?"

"Yes."

"I'm Mr. Mesurier's secretary." She gave an unexpectedly attractive smile. "He's on his way down from a meeting, and he may just be a minute or two late."

"I'm early," Gideon declared.

"Oh, are you?" She sounded surprised, but he had a feeling that she had been fully aware of it.

She led him past the clatter and ringing, all the perpetrators hidden by the frosted-glass walls which were little more than partitions, into a room at the far end of the passage marked "NEWS EDITOR," in black, on a solid oak door. As the door closed on Gideon and the woman, the noise was shut out; for a split second absolute silence reigned in the room, a small, square one, with an old, richly colored carpet and a Chesterfield suite in dark green, worn a little at the arms but comfortable-looking. In the middle of the room was a round table on a pedestal, with magazines and newspapers neatly set out. A door, closed, led to Mesurier's office, where Gideon had been once before at a time of acute pressure in the relationship between the press and the police. At that time, Mesurier had been a representative of a journalists' association.

A small star-shaped electric clock on the wall seemed slightly inappropriate. It said twenty-five past two. Gideon sat in one of the armchairs, which was comfortably large enough, and picked up a copy of the *Daily News*. He saw a short paragraph about the newspaper strike, a column about the dock strike, and two main stories—one about a British ship lost at sea, and the other about an Air France jet-plane crash killing a hundred and seven people in the Pyrenees.

The inner door opened and Mesurier came in.

He was a man of medium height, with a lean body and a narrow face, short-cut hair, fine brown eyes. His lips were full, somehow not in keeping with the rest of his face, and he had a pointed chin. He was immaculate in a pale brown suit.

"Commander, how good to see you after so long." The words were right even if the tone lacked warmth; the handclasp was firm enough. "Please come in." He stood aside for Gideon to enter a room at least twice as long as the outer room, book-lined wherever bookshelves could be squeezed, with a large desk of mahogany and trays also of dark wood. It had the air of a scholar's room, nothing of the controlled bustle of a newspaper editor's. A companion suite to the one in the other room was at the far end, and Mesurier motioned to one of the chairs, then sat opposite Gideon; he seemed lost in the big chair.

Mesurier always left the opening move to the other man, and it could make one uncomfortable and ill-at-ease.

Gideon said, "I would like your advice and probably your help."

"That sounds most intriguing."

"In a very tricky and potentially dangerous situation," Gideon went on.

"Dangerous to . . ." Mesurier allowed the "to" to hover, and gave no help at all. There was no expression on his face, no twist or curve to his lips.

"All of us," Gideon stated.

"I see," said Mesurier quietly. "Presumably, you mean the dock troubles."

"Yes, I do."

"I would have expected a politician to come and discuss it, or else industrialists who fear the effect of a strike," Mesurier remarked. "But not you, or any policeman."

Could there be the slightest hint of reproof in his voice? Or was this just an unfortunate manner? It made Gideon wonder whether he had been right to come to this man; like the lift, the man's attitude made him feel very slightly apprehensive. And there was still time to switch themes, not to confide.

"Don't have any doubts, I'm here because I'm a policeman," Gideon told him gruffly. "May I be sure that everything I say will be held in complete confidence?"

"Yes," Mesurier answered.

"Thank you." Gideon settled back in his chair, stretched out his legs, and crossed his ankles. He weighed his words for a few moments and then went on: "I have information from what I believe to be a reliable source that a group of right-wingers—extreme right-wingers—calling themselves the Strike Breakers, plan to break up the dock-gate meetings which have been called for tomorrow at noon." He went on to tell Mesurier all he had learned from Lawless and Sir Giles without going into too much detail and without naming either man. All the time, he looked into Mesurier's expressionless face. Those fine eyes were half hidden now, by lids which drooped, while his mouth seemed thinner, as if he were pursing his lips. Disapprovingly? Suddenly, a new thought flashed: Mesurier might already know about the Strike Breakers, might even have decided on a course of action.

Gideon finished, and they sat in silence. Gideon remembered once sitting with the Minister of Power a few years ago, and having a similar kind of feeling: that he was getting nowhere, that he might as well stand up and leave. But he sat there as if fully relaxed, prepared to wait a long time for Mesurier to speak. He noticed that the other man had a plain gold band on his wedding finger, and he reflected that he knew nothing at all about Mesurier's personal life.

At last, Mesurier spoke.

"And you suggest that if the story is leaked at the right time, the police can take some kind of quick action, without appearing at the docks so early that the dockers feel you're after them alone. However, you want to keep the Strike Breakers from attacking effectively, but they would be allowed to assemble and show their hand so you could charge anyone who attempted violence. You want them to assemble because you want to know their strength and to find out who their leaders are."

"That's it precisely," Gideon agreed. He felt much better. This man comprehended the situation absolutely.

"You know we've a complete shutdown threatening in Fleet Street, too, don't you?"

"Yes."

"Supposing we don't get a paper out tomorrow?"

"Is it really as serious as that?"

"Yes," Mesurier answered flatly.

"Then I would have to use B.B.C. radio."

For the first time, Mesurier smiled and his eyes lit up; and, for the first time, Gideon felt completely at ease. Moreover, he felt a lot of admiration for this man, bedeviled by the possibility of a strike of his own printers, yet agreeing so promptly to see him.

"You've really thought it through," Mesurier said. "Are others with you on this?"

Gideon didn't answer, and Mesurier's smile became almost droll.

"I see. Well, of course I can help; I can help perhaps two ways. I will have a stop-press item in the morning's paper if we get out; on the other hand, if it's obvious we're not going to, then I've a newsroom contact at the B.B.C. who will put this little tidbit out for me. There is one other thing I would like to do. I'd like to send a man down to the docks at once."

"Wouldn't you, normally?" asked Gideon.

"Not until the dock-gate meetings were about to start— dock troubles have been going on for so long that they're not exactly headline news until they really erupt in some way or other. If I send a man down to make a few inquiries now, then it will look more natural when we break the story. And I'd like to find out whether the dockers have any intimation of a threat from these Strike Breakers."

Gideon said heavily, "I see."

"Does it worry you?" asked Mesurier.

"I wouldn't like your man to draw attention to the possibility of trouble," Gideon said.

"You would have no need at all to worry. I'd make sure he knew exactly what he had to do, and if he discovered anything I would inform you. I would not use anything without your specific agreement. Is that satisfactory?"

"Perfectly," Gideon answered, all his reservations broken down. "I can't thank you enough."

He did not know why, but something in those heartfelt words affected Mesurier and his expression again became one that could be taken for disapproval. Certainly there was nothing commonplace about this man or his reactions. Gideon waited in the uncomfortable silence, having been given all he could have hoped for, watching the other but sitting upright now, and probably looking no more relaxed than he was. Slowly, Mesurier leaned forward and spread his hands, gesture and expression both of resignation.

"Commander," he said, "have you the faintest idea how privileged I feel that of all the men in Fleet Street who could have helped in this matter, you selected me? I am very—moved. And more than moved: I am deeply impressed. Like everyone on the Street, I have long had a great respect for you as the one policeman who will come to us on equal terms—never trying even remotely to use police or Home Office pressure. I doubt if you have any idea how many friends you have in this strange, closed world of ours. If we'd needed any telling, the Notting Hill affair and your concern for those immigrants showed your compassion as a human being. Now this—" He spread his hands again and smiled more widely but with some tension, perhaps suppressing an emotion he did not want to show. "What usually appalls me is how few people, even in high positions in all fields of endeavor, ever see beyond the immediate situation. You and your anonymous friends see that, clumsily handled, this situation could lead to acute bad feeling in the docks and make all the difference between a strike and no strike. Possibly between hunger and sufficiency for some; even between success and failure in the nation's economy. And you—well, you are one of those few men."

Gideon, who was at first startled, then warmed, finally felt a touch of embarrassment. He marveled that he had assessed this man both so rightly and so wrongly, and spread his own big hands and said gruffly, "But surely those things are all obvious."

"Obvious?" echoed Mesurier. "Glaringly obvious, yes, Commander. God, how right the simple axioms are—how difficult it is to see the wood for the trees! Commander, sometimes I think the morons are right, that we would be better off if we grabbed everything we could for ourselves and devil take the hindmost. Tell me, do *you* know whether a man without a conscience is as happy and untroubled as he often seems to be? Do *you* know why a man with a conscience is always likely to be more worried, troubled, anguished—"

He broke off.

He pressed his hands against the sides of his head, as if he wanted to squeeze himself to silence. He sat like that for only a few seconds, and then he took his hands away and spoke with a comical expression on his face.

"I'm sorry, Commander. Truly sorry. I had just come from a meeting of employers where the nicest of men, the most honest of men, were as obdurate and unseeing as morons. And this morning I had a meeting with some of the union leaders—just as nice, just as honest, just as obdurate and unseeing. I had expected you to want cooperation in some campaign against crime of great importance but to me secondary—do forgive me. And instead I find you a farseeing police officer—obviously one of several. In my enthusiasm, I talked too much. Do forgive me."

"Nothing to forgive," mumbled Gideon. "I will admit you shook me a bit, but I know exactly what you mean."

"I know you do," Mesurier said. "And I should have realized it before. At least be sure that I'll do what I've promised with very real pleasure." He got up, and Gideon rose slowly, hesitated, and then as they went toward the door, he asked, "Do you really think you're in for a strike, Mr. Mesurier?" He pronounced the name "Mesur-i-ay." "Or can you avoid it?"

"I've a most uneasy feeling that the best we can do is postpone it," Mesurier answered. "And if it has to come I'm not really convinced that it wouldn't be better to have it now."

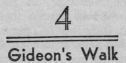

4

Gideon's Walk

GIDEON LEFT the offices of the *Daily News,* caught his driver's eye, and beckoned him, and when the man came up, he said, "Meet me along by Somerset House—the widest part of the Strand. I may be half an hour." He was still glowing from much that Mesurier had said.

"Right, sir."

"Any messages?"

"Not for you yourself, sir."

"Anything noteworthy?" asked Gideon.

"There's been a very big bullion robbery at London Airport, sir."

"Hmm," grunted Gideon, and turned left along Fleet Street and toward the Strand, while the driver went off to his car, which would be parked somewhere nearby when Gideon reappeared.

Had there been any urgent need for him, Hobbs, his deputy, would have put out a call, although these days Gideon was needed less and less in the routine running of the Criminal Investigation Department. Hobbs did a great deal of the briefing and liaising, which eased a little of the pressure for Gideon. The danger, he knew, was that Hobbs might do too much, but he was fifteen years Gideon's junior and there wasn't much danger he'd overdo things.

Gideon wanted to walk.

His old manor was the West End, including Soho, and

he had never known Fleet Street and the nearby area as
well. Yet he knew it well enough, and associated it with
the big national newspapers: the *Telegraph,* the *Express,*
and the *Mail,* the *Sun* of checkered history, the *Mirror,*
and, of course, the Sunday papers. He always had to be
reminded that Fleet Street was no longer the street of the
newspaper giants. Only the *Telegraph* and the *Express*
were actually housed here, while Fleet Street itself seemed
to belong more to the provincial press. He walked past
so many familiar names. The Wolverhampton *Express
& Star,* the Birmingham *Mail,* the Sheffield *Star,* the
Western Morning News—there they were, with tiny offices in this so-called Street of Ink, linking with all the
major cities of the land; indeed, of all the world. And
there were thrice as many names unknown to him as there
were familiar ones. In some windows and doorways, the
legend told of the Sydney *Morning Herald* and the Cape
Town *Argus,* the Montreal *Standard* and the Westmorland
Gazette. From these, from the great agencies, the wires
were buzzing, teletypes tapping, across the lands and across
the oceans, carrying news from London to the world, and
bringing it from the farthermost parts of the earth to
London.

Yet the giants were not here.

If he walked down Fetter Lane, he'd come eventually
to Holborn, where the *Mirror* and *Sunday Mirror* had
their mammoth modern homes. In the opposite direction
and much nearer to St. Paul's, though hidden from it,
was the *Times,* in Printing House Square: the "old
Thunderer," as he could well remember it being called.
Newspapers seemed often to scream and shout and bellow
but seldom to thunder nowadays. Much farther off, beyond the *Mirror,* was the Thomson Empire in Gray's
Inn Road, with the *Sunday Times* across the road, as it
were, from the near Elysian fields of Gray's Inn itself,
close to its grass and trees. And, closer to him as well
as to Fleet Street, big old buildings between here and the

river housed the *Mail* and the *Sketch,* the *Evening News,* and the *News of the World* and the *People.*

There were far fewer papers than there had once been, but still a goodly number.

And they might all soon be off the streets because of the strike.

As he walked with long deliberate stride, oblivious of the fact that many people moved out of his way, he found himself thinking again of the parallel he had formed in his mind that morning between the newspapers with their cargoes of words and the ships with their cargoes of food and goods and the wherewithal of life. Food for the body, food for the mind.

He gave a sudden snort of a laugh.

I'm taking myself too seriously, he thought; I was even before Mesurier let forth, and after that I need a new size in hats!

He shook himself free of these reflections, and, glancing across a traffic-free stretch of the narrow road, saw a man on the other side who had been in prison until a few years ago: a very clever forger. Suddenly, Fleet Street seemed alive not with ideas but with people.

He saw one of the best-known columnists in England.

He saw Wilde, the Court Photographer.

He recognized Tiffen, the crime reporter of some of the A.P. group, and Raphael, managing director of one of the biggest advertising agencies.

This became a street not simply of newspaper names from home and abroad but also of photographs in windows—action photographs of film stars, politicians, the docks, footballers, cricketers, fashion models, small homes, and stately homes. It became a reflection not simply of news from all over the world but of a huge gossip column. He was smiling to himself now. Here were the hurrying crowds, the young and the old, the pictures and the newspapers, the—

"It is Commander Gideon, isn't it?" a man said from behind him. He turned to see a tall, willowy, long-haired man with very clear-cut features; he recognized Nigel Simply, of the *Globe*, perhaps the most renowned of all the gossip columnists. "It *is*," Simply said. "Do please tell me what you're doing in Fleet Street, Commander."

"What would you expect me to be doing?" asked Gideon mildly.

Simply had beautifully shaped rosy lips. His complexion was nearly perfect—in fact, appeared to have a bloom. His pale brown eyes smiled easily.

"Looking for bad men," he answered.

"As always," Gideon agreed.

"The noncommittal Commander!"

"As a policeman, I have to be noncommittal."

"Dare I ask if you're after any particular bad man?" asked Simply.

Gideon answered, smiling faintly, "Yes, but I daren't tell you who."

"Commander—" The other's voice took on a feathery tone.

"Yes?"

"Could you possibly spare time for a cup of tea?"

"And some questions?"

"Well, yes, but not forbidden ones," Simply promised. "I haven't had a policeman in the column for a long time—since Sir Giles Rook was appointed to the City, in fact." Could that remark be more than sheer coincidence? "And do you know, I don't think I've ever done a piece about you."

"I hope you never will," Gideon replied, half smiling.

"Oh, come. I can be most rewarding."

"Yes, I know," Gideon said. "And devastating."

"Only to those who attempt to deceive me. I've a club near here, a small one for select members of Fleet Street," urged Simply. "At least come and have some tea with me. The—ah—image of the police could always be improved, couldn't it?"

"I'm sorry," Gideon said, "but I haven't time now.

Though I've nothing against being interviewed, in principle."

"You have to ask permission," suggested Simply.

Gideon felt a flare of annoyance; felt, too, that this man was deliberately needling him, perhaps because Gideon had almost fallen to the temptation of being written up in his "Simply Speaking" column. But there was no point in showing annoyance, and there might be a lot of good in parting on unbarbed terms. Simply was smiling a rather set smile.

"Well, of course," Gideon said. "Anyone who is interviewed by Nigel Simply knows that he might be lured into indiscretions, so I'd have to get my absolution in advance—as well as ponder what I want to say."

"You mean you will let me interview you?"

"Of course. If you're serious."

"You don't know how serious, Commander! You wouldn't like to say, off the cuff, what you think about the Fleet Street strike, would you?" Simply asked blandly.

"It's a great pity when any channel of communication is blocked," Gideon replied easily.

Simply placed a hand on his shoulder and squeezed gently, said "I do agree," and walked back the way he had come. Gideon went on, more slowly. It was just possible that the question about the strike and the remark about Rook were in some way significant, but he thought it much more likely that Simply had come upon him by chance and hurried up for a word.

Of course, Simply *might* have seen him come out of the *Daily News* office.

And supposing he had, Gideon thought, what difference would it make? When one paid a visit in confidence, it was easy to imagine all kinds of leakages. Just as Fleet Street was the place for news, so it was the place for gossip and rumor, with Nigel Simply the most inveterate and often most malicious gossip of them all.

Gideon tried to put the encounter out of his mind.

His driver was waiting and he was back at the Yard a

little before four o'clock. A note on his desk told him that
Alec Hobbs would be in about half past five, and as had
become normal, Alec had put the files of various cases
on his desk, together with notes about them and the men
handling each one. Gideon opened the first file, marked
"Smith, P. J.—Murder." It was a long gloomy record of
the sad story of a man who some time ago had killed his
wife and two sons and then gone on the run from the police. He hadn't yet been found, and Gideon and others
at the Yard thought he had probably killed himself. So
far, no body which might have been his had been
discovered.

Gideon opened the file to see a note from Hobbs at-
tached to the photograph of a man who might conceivably
be Smith—alive, very much alive. Hobbs's note said:
"Taken in Sydney, New South Wales," and Gideon studied
it with fresh interest. There was another note: "This photograph was taken in the Sydney Easter Fair by a newspaper
photographer who noticed a similarity to a picture he had
seen in an English newspaper eighteen months ago."
"Good Lord!" exclaimed Gideon. There on the back was
the photographer's name, as well as the approximate date
of the English newspaper. Hobbs had added: "Am checking." Gideon put this aside, feeling a sharp thrill of excitement. If it was the same man, then they certainly wanted
him! He picked up the next, much slimmer folder. Here
were some reports from Division and some photographs
of a bank safe which had been blown the previous night.
So far, there were no clues. Next was a very slim folder
which carried only a note from Hobbs.

2:47 P.M. First report from Heathrow Airport of a
consignment of gold (bullion) from South Africa
shipped on an S.A. Airways VC–10 and being hi-
jacked after unloading. Airport, Hounslow Staines,
and ourselves collaborating. I may need to go to
Heathrow myself.

That was probably where he had gone, Gideon reflected. He picked up the next folder and went absolutely still, for the name on it was Entwhistle, a man who had served nearly four years of a life sentence for a murder he had not committed. The case had been reopened and Entwhistle had been granted the Queen's pardon.

Why was the folder back?

Gideon opened it and saw a photograph of a smiling Entwhistle and his three children, and on the back a note signed by Entwhistle and saying:

> We are off to Australia in a few weeks. I hope you will keep this as a memento. I shall never be able to begin to thank you.

Supposing he, Gideon, had not reopened the case? Supposing— He closed the folder slowly. As he did so, a curious thing happened: he seemed to see the face of Nigel Simply hovering in front of his mind's eye. Immediately he was jerked out of the past and into the urgent, pressing present. Without a moment's hesitation, he picked up one of three telephones, the one connected with the Yard's exchange, and ordered: "Get me Mr. Mesurier of the *Daily News*."

"Right, sir."

There was a long delay, and during it he reflected on what had happened during the day and on what he had done, as well as what needed doing. Suddenly he thought, I should let Rook and Lawless know about this. But before he went beyond that the exchange telephone rang.

"Mr. Mesurier, sir."

"Thank you. Mr. Mesurier?"

"Yes, Commander?"

"This is a trifle but you might think it worth knowing," Gideon said. "Nigel Simply caught up with me soon after I left you, and asked one or two questions which made me wonder whether, in fact, he'd seen me come from your offices, or else been told. Do you think it could have any significance?"

Mesurier did not answer at once.

It wasn't lack of interest, Gideon was sure; the silence lasted for a long time before Mesurier answered.

"With that man the most trifling incident can become significant, but in this case no one else can possibly know why you came to see me. Of course, there is the possibility that when Simply sees the stop-press and realizes that you may possibly have been our source of information, he may put a note in his column. That would do me no harm. Would it affect you?"

"Provided it doesn't concern the docks situation, no."

"I can't see how it can possibly do that," Mesurier said. He paused again, and when he went on his voice had changed slightly. "I've already briefed a man to go to the docks. One of our feature writers, not just a reporter. He will do a piece more or less along the lines of my outburst this afternoon. If there's anything unusual going on, he'll find out."

"Good," said Gideon, and stopped himself from saying "thanks."

"Thanks for calling," replied Mesurier, and rang off.

5

Offensive Weapons

MALCOLM BRILL of the *Daily News* was frowning as he
came out of the news editor's office. He was a small,
fair-haired, myriad-freckled man, with innocent-seeming
pale green eyes, and it was often said that he had the look
of an Irishman, although there was no known Irish blood
in his ancestry. Perhaps because he was so small and
fair, he seemed young, and so made people talk much
more freely than they intended. Many were astonished
later at how much they had said to him. There was, however, no spite and no malice in him and, like all the best
journalists, he was utterly reliable: if he was told a thing
"off the record," it was completely safe with him.

Some said this was why he had refused many offers
from the giants, and stayed with the *News;* he was, in
effect, his own boss there. It was not, however, his only
reason for staying.

The second reason was his wife.

He loved his wife.

She was, to him, very beautiful. She mattered to him
more than any other human being in the world, and that
did not except their two children. On the staff of the
News, he could lead a more orderly life than on some
bigger newspapers, where he would be—he thought
rightly—at the editor's beck and call. In a way, of course,
he was at Mesurier's beck and call, but the news editor
used his authority with reason and understanding. More-

43

over, the paper could not afford to send him to the ends of the earth at short notice with a virtual carte blanche for an expense account. Consequently, Brill could usually rely on being home at a reasonable hour, and in cases where he had to put in a late story he could telephone it from home.

Only now and again did Mesurier give him a job which might keep him out late; that was why, when Mesurier briefed him on the docks job, there simply wasn't any way of putting it off or asking for someone else to do it. Mesurier had made it clear that he considered Brill the only man for the job.

So Malcolm Brill would spend the rest of the day at the docks, and as a dock day really lasted twenty-four hours, there was no possible way of being sure what time he would get home—almost certainly after the pubs closed and he had wormed his last confidence out of a docker whose tongue had been loosened by too many beers.

He would have to telephone Rose and tell her he couldn't go to Covent Garden tonight. The Bolshoi Ballet was making one of its rare visits and its selection from the repertoire was to be *Swan Lake*. Only by exerting all his influence on the *News*'s performing-arts critic had Brill been able to get tickets, carrying them home in triumph one evening last week. A sitter had been arranged, and Rose had bought new shoes, a new evening handbag, and evening gloves, for tonight was a very great occasion.

Now he was going to have to tell her he couldn't go.

He flinched at the very thought.

A telephone call would be too cold and distant; he would have to go and see her. There was just time, although if he did the job as he wanted to, he would go straight out to the docks and have a breather about six o'clock. He couldn't wait that long to break the news. If there was only someone who could go in his place, it would solve the main problem. He wasn't fool or vain enough to believe it would make too much difference if he wasn't there; missing the brilliant occasion would hurt Rose more.

He opened a door in the partition-type walls, and the noise became suddenly bedlam. Every inch of space at the *News* desk was in use. The desk was set in a square, three reporters on each outside section, one sub on each inside section; two assistant news editors—presentation, not policy, men—were at a large desk adjoining. Typewriters rattled like machine guns—except Maisie White's. Maisie, young, lumpy, coarse-haired, was the worst typist of them all but also as good a reporter as any. She had nice big gray eyes, and they were raised from the old machine toward him. They focused. He waved a mock salute and passed on. His was one of six small desks at the end of the room, each with its own telephone, typewriter, filing cabinet, desk armchair, plus a chair for the features man and, at the far end, one for a girl from the big typists' pool. Only a very few top men at the *News* had their own secretary; and many in the pool were little more than copy typists. He sat down, still wondering who could stand in for him.

It would have to be someone Rose knew and liked.

Who?

It would have to be someone from the office, or someone he could get in touch with quickly. It was now nearly four o'clock; Rose was probably beginning to get her things ready, spreading them out on the bed and gloating over them.

He had a bachelor cousin who might escort Rose, and Rose had a brother who was living apart from his wife. Either might help him out. He put in a call to his cousin, only to be told by a secretary that he was out of town; and to his brother-in-law, who said no regretfully—he had a club meeting and, as secretary, had to be present.

As he rang off, Brill was aware of someone approaching, and of a shadow over the desk, and he half turned to see Maisie. With part of his mind he wished her a thousand miles away, with the other he welcomed her; she was the one person at the office with whom he could talk.

"Hallo, Maisie."

"Hi, Malcolm. Been fired?"

"Not yet," he said. "Do I look as if I had?"

"To Maisie's discerning eye, yes."

"Well, Maisie's discerning eye discerned wrong for once."

"Half wrong," she retorted, sitting in the secretary's chair.

"The half that discerned I am not the happiest of souls this afternoon? All right, half-discerning eye. And as I'd been called to King Charles you thought I'd been banished. No." He hesitated, never a man to wear his heart on his sleeve, and then found himself saying ruefully, "No. *He* wants the human story behind the dockers. A new slant worthy of that part of the *News* which is like the *Guardian*. And he wants it for tomorrow morning, because tomorrow night might be after the event. I mean, strike. So, I'm to go off now."

"Oh," said Maisie, as if her heart had dropped, too. "So you can't take Rose to the ball?"

"Ballet, really. No." He looked at Maisie with new interest, and actually sat up straight. "Are *you* free?"

"I can just imagine Rose's face if I were to appear all dressed up and ready to say let's go! No, Mal, I would gladly go if I thought it would help, but you know it wouldn't. On such an occasion Rose would need a male escort; anything else would be"—she paused as if checking a word, and then went on—"disappointing. No one would really replace you, of course."

"But a handsome and dashing substitute would help, you mean?"

"A respectable male, anyway."

"Name one," urged Malcolm Brill.

She had a trick, when she was thinking, of looking away from whoever was with her; it was a form of concentration. She had a round head, short, black hair, a short neck, and a very white skin, and she nearly always wore a dress which showed a wide expanse and a hint of cleavage. Today her dress was black and the cleavage deeper than usual.

She stared past him for a long time, and then looked back and said briskly, "Jack Ledden."

"Who?"

"Jack Ledden—from advertising."

"Good lord!" Malcolm exclaimed. "You mean—" He broke off, seeing in his mind's eye the man Maisie had thought of and whom he had completely forgotten. Back in December, at the *News* ball, Ledden had been one of a party which had haphazardly gathered in a corner and become virtually isolated from the rest. He did not remember how Ledden had happened to join a group which was mostly editorial, but he remembered Ledden's girl friend had come from accounting. Ledden was also active in the social activities of the staff, and played on the cricket and football teams. He was a tall, pleasant, nice-looking man in his thirties.

"I mean Jack Ledden."

"Do you know him?"

"Yes. I'm on the committee of the social club, too."

"If I remember rightly," Malcolm said, "Rose danced with him several times."

"Yes," Maisie said dryly. "I believe she did."

"But I hardly know him!"

"Like me to telephone him?" asked Maisie, and even as she spoke she leaned across for the interoffice telephone. She had a full and beautiful bosom, but Brill was completely oblivious of it. She dialed an extension obviously familiar to her, and only when there was a break in the ringing sound did he mutter, "Oh, you might as well."

"Jack," Maisie said. "Maisie . . . Yes, wasn't it. . . . No, I can't manage Friday. . . . Are you doing anything tonight? . . . You can easily put that off, can't you?" Maisie laughed lightly. "A very good reason—you can

help a friend of mine. . . . Do you remember Malcolm
Brill? . . . I thought you might! He has an assignment
which he can't break and so can't take his wife to the
ballet tonight—a really big night, black tie and all that.
. . . He's sitting here with me, hold on." Maisie pressed
the mouthpiece to her bosom and whispered to Malcolm,
"He was going to play table tennis, but I know he's not
keen, and he'd be glad to have an excuse to put it off.
Have a word with him."

Malcolm took the receiver and said, in a curiously
choky voice, "I know this is an infernal nerve, but if you
could possibly stand in for me . . ."

By the time he finished, Maisie had gone back to her
chair at the *News* desk. She was hunting and pecking at
the typewriter with greater vigor than usual, and didn't
look up when he passed.

He went straight downstairs, and two taxis approached
with their signs alight. He got the first, ordered "Mallet
Street, Camberwell," and sat back. He still could not be
sure how Rose would take it, and had some misgivings
now; perhaps he should have checked with her first.

There simply hadn't been time.

There was the Pool, the most romantic part of the great
Port of London, with ships being worked as if there were
no thought that in two days they might be standing idle.
As the taxi turned toward Camberwell Green, it passed
the bank which had been robbed only the previous night,
and almost at the same time, two jet aircraft flew over
carrying passengers and cargo, including gold bullion, to
Heathrow Airport. Brill was too preoccupied to do what
he normally did: go through recent big stories in his mind,
wondering whether any feature of them had been missed,
whether one could be used in the *News*. When the taxi
pulled up outside the row of small, new terraced houses,
built on the site of an old building damaged by bombing,
he saw Dorothy, his younger child, at the window. Her
face lit up, and he saw but did not hear her call, "Daddy!
Daddy!"

When he opened the front door, she was in the passage, jumping up and down with joy at seeing him. She was four, fair-haired, dressed in a pair of pants a shade too tight for her. He hoisted her above his head and tossed her two or three times, while she giggled and gurgled. His other child, eleven-year-old Roger, was probably not home from school.

"Malcolm!" Rose called from upstairs. "Is that you?"

"Yes, sweet, I—"

"Can you take Dot to the Adamses? Roger's going straight there. They're going to stay the night. I'm terribly behind with everything!"

"I'll take her," Malcolm promised. "But—"

"Send her up to say goodbye," called Rose, and Dorothy went scrambling up the stairs. There was laughing and voices saying, "Be good," and "Have a nice time," until at last she was downstairs again. The Adamses lived only a few minutes away. Dot skipped happily along, Malcolm carrying the small suitcase which had the children's nightclothes. Paula Adams, hot from cooking, offered him a cup of tea, but he said no, he must get back.

"I'm so glad you could get home early," Paula said. "Rose is so excited about it, she's bound to be all fingers and thumbs."

He forced a smile and said, "I'll bet she will be."

The house was silent when he got back; strangely so. He called, but got no answer. There was really very little time—he must get to the docks—so he called her as he hurried up the stairs. Then he heard water running and realized she was in the bath. The door was ajar and steam curled out onto the landing.

"Rose!" he called.

"I won't be long!" she called back.

He pushed open the door and went in as she was stepping into the tub. She was—beautiful. He loved her body so. There were problems in the marriage and one of them was that she liked to bathe "in private," and indeed liked much more privacy than was common between husband

and wife. But if she was fastidious, why shouldn't she be?

Now, lowering herself into the bath, she said crossly, "You know I don't like anyone with me when I'm bathing."

"I know," he said. "But I have to speak to you."

"Anything can wait—"

"No, it can't," Malcolm said, more sharply than he usually spoke to her. "I shouldn't be here at all. I've an assignment I can't possibly refuse tonight. I—"

He broke off, for she looked absolutely horrified, so affected that she crouched there, arms raised, body misted by the steam, her expression such that for the first time in their lives he became oblivious of her body, of her beauty.

In a strident voice, she cried, "You mean we can't *go*."

"No, I mean *I* can't but you can," he said. "I hadn't time to consult you so I arranged with a friend at the office to take you. You've met him, and—well, anyhow, there wasn't any choice. It was either this or you going alone, and—"

"And just who *is* this creature who is to stand in for my husband?" Rose demanded shrilly.

Malcolm said brusquely, "Jack Ledden. You met and liked him at the *News* ball. He'll call for you at half past six, and will take you to dinner before the ballet. I hope you don't hate him, but it was the best I could do."

Before she could speak again, he went out and closed the door.

6

The Docker

IT WAS half past six when Malcolm Brill turned in to The
Docker, a public house near the gates of the Victoria and
Albert Docks. The high dock walls were of gray stone,
and police guarded all the entrances—the Metropolitan
Police outside, the Port of London Authority Police inside.
Although it was autonomous, the P.L.A. force worked
very closely with Gideon's men. Inside the docks were
roads and railway tracks and warehouses, all much the
same as they had been a hundred years ago; even the
roads were unchanged except for resurfacing. Many of
the warehouses were nearly derelict and the tall cranes
were old.

But The Docker was a modern building of red brick and
contemporary design, with a psychedelic inn sign. About it
were tall modern buildings, blocks of flats, and some two-
and single-story houses, all built within the last five years.
The docks were like an oasis of yesterday in the red and
yellow bricks, the concrete, and the bright paint of today.
Another sign of the times was the presence of dozens of
cars parked on the docks, mostly old cars but a few new
and shiny. There were no more than half a dozen bicycles,
whereas in the days when the original Docker had been
built, which the present one had replaced, there would
have been fifty or sixty.

Malcolm Brill, who had come by tube and bus, went
into the Four Ale bar. He wore an old felt hat and a

shabby tweed suit. As he entered the big, square, smoke-filled room, he saw one man pass another man something which looked as if it were made of brass and had holes in it. A third man was wrapping a length of cycle chain in an oily rag; he slipped the packet into his bulging coat pocket as the stranger came in.

A man was saying, "And we'll give the buggers as good as—"

Someone whispered, "Shut up!"

"What's got into you?" the first man demanded.

"Just keep your trap shut," the second said.

There was no doubt at all that his, Brill's, arrival had caused that abrupt piece of dialogue; equally no doubt that a silence fell upon the room as Brill moved toward the long bar.

Someone laughed on a high note; someone else said, "What's the price on Fairo?"

"Tens," someone answered.

"I'll put a quid on her to win."

"Okay, quid to win, Fairo."

Brill reached the bar. He had been here before and recognized some of the men, including a big fellow with a pale face and a broken nose, wearing, incongruously, a pair of gold-rimmed pince-nez: Willis Murdoch of the London Dock Workers' Union.

Brill ordered, "Half of bitter, please."

"Half of bitter—okay."

"Thanks." The small tankard changed hands, the head overflowing down the glass sides. Brill drank. He noticed several men take their hands, empty, out of their pockets; and he also noticed that many pockets bulged, whether in old coats and jackets or in new. There were some lumps against the blue, gray, and black sweaters, too, as if a bulky object had been tucked underneath. A man laughed. One asked, "Think we'll be able to afford a pint next week, Jim?" Another replied, "You telling me you can afford it this week, Charlie?" That brought more laughter and there was a general return to conversation, mostly about the strike.

"Think the bosses will up any more?"

"Not a stinking penny."

"They've got to or we'll be out."

"They don't see it that way."

"Stand firm, that's my motto," remarked a man who sounded as if he'd had plenty of beer already.

"Gotta come to terms sooner or later," a small man observed. "Why not sooner?"

"The flickers never do."

"I don't mind telling you I'm against the strike," another man declared. "It will only mean more trouble in the long run. We ought to be reasonable—that's what I say."

"Put a sock in it, Micky!"

"Reasonable! How reasonable do you think I feel when I take home fifteen quid to feed six?"

"Don't forget the family allowance, Sammy boy!"

"Buy your missus a pill, Sammy!"

The guffaws which followed that sally brought the atmosphere back much nearer to normal, and Brill moved farther from the bar. Willis Murdoch was standing with his back to him, and Brill edged toward him. Then he saw a youthful-looking, very slim man over in a corner, talking to two dockers. The man wore large horn-rimmed glasses, and a lock of dark hair fell over his forehead and was lodged between his eyes and the lenses; he kept pushing it back. Brill recognized him as a reporter on the North Thames *Times,* one of a group of weekly newspapers which served an area stretching from Aldgate Pump to East Ham. This particular man was a stringer for a number of provincial and some other London weeklies and also turned in an occasional story for the national dailies. Something in his manner suggested he was scared, but he was probably putting on an act.

Brill turned from him toward Murdoch, who was saying, in his rough voice, "We'll come out if we have to and we won't if we don't."

"Good old Willis," a man applauded ironically. "You always know where you stand with Willis."

"Do you, Mr. Murdoch?" Brill asked the dockers' leader.

Murdoch turned slowly and deliberately and looked down on him. The pince-nez could give the pale face a sneering, supercilious expression, and never more so than now. Brill was quite sure that he had been recognized and that this was simply an act; Murdoch wanted to make the newspaperman look small.

"And who are *you?*"

Brill answered crisply, "My name is Malcolm Brill, I'm from the *Daily News*." He spoke so clearly that a lot of people nearby heard and there was another, briefer silence, which lasted until a man said, "A bloody newspaperman!"

"That's right," agreed Brill.

"We don't want you Fleet Street so-and-sos here," called someone out of sight.

"Too bloody true we don't!"

"Why don't you hop it, mate?"

"Take a powder."

"Come sneaking in here—" A big man with reddish hair spoke in a rough Irish brogue. "Why, we ought to smash his face in."

In that moment, Brill thought that the speaker had everyone with him; he had never been more aware of hostility in a crowd and it did not console him to know that someone else had engendered the hostility. He had a curious thought: that they might beat him up and throw him out—literally—if Willis Murdoch gave the word or sign. On an evening when his own mood was so brittle, when the way he had disappointed Rose tormented him, he felt unable to cope. He had never before been called on to cope in any such emergency. He should not have come. He should have refused the assignment; even if Mesurier had forced the issue—do the job or leave the paper—he should have insisted. No newspaper owned a man.

He did not know how he managed to find his normal voice. "You don't have to answer questions and you don't have to have your case put before the public. That's up to you. But I didn't 'come sneaking in here,' as you put it. I came in by the main door and ordered my own beer." He drained the tankard and placed it carefully on the bar. "Same again," he said to the worried-looking man behind the bar. For the first time, he noticed that the barman had only one arm.

Willis Murdoch said, "Have that one on me, mate. What did you say your name was?"

"Brill. Malcolm Brill."

"And you watch your step, Red," Murdoch said to the Irishman. "We don't want any trouble in here with anyone, least of all the national press. And Mr. Brill's right, he didn't sneak in." He took the replenished tankard from the bar and thrust it, handle first, toward Brill. "What's this about presenting our case to the public?"

"That's what I'm here to try to do."

"Two-thirds for the bosses, a third for us, highly colored —is that it?" Murdoch raised his glass. "Cheers." He drank.

"Cheers." Brill sipped, but didn't drink much. "Is that how the newspaper reports seem to you?"

"Yes," Murdoch answered.

"Crooked all the way," put in a man from behind him.

"Paid by the bosses, if you ask me," another said.

"There's only one way to put your case, and that's to do it ourselves," a third declared. "Old Homer, over there, he was born one of us, he's been around as long as I have, but do you think he can do a piece of good honest reporting?" The speaker was in his middle thirties, wearing a waisted jacket of pale green suède and a frilled pink shirt. He had curly hair, a shade overlong.

"I've been here five minutes," Brill countered. "I came to try to get an objective story. So far, you've done little

but make me anti-docker. One man threatened to bash
my face in, and if it wasn't for Mr. Murdoch, maybe he
would have tried. The next thing, all you seem interested
in is attacking newspapers. What do you expect as a result? Me to go out of here and write a piece about our
wonderful dockers?"

Silence fell, while Murdoch looked down on him, the
Irishman formed words but did not utter them, and Brill
realized that old Homer was the man in the horn-rimmed
glasses. Then someone laughed.

"Straight from the shoulder," he said. "You've got to
admit that."

"Hear, hear," chimed in another. "He's got guts."

"Words can be twisted, that's what I say," muttered the
Irishman.

"All right, Mr. Brill," said Murdoch, finishing his beer,
"you ask the questions and we'll answer them. And when
this piece of yours appears, we'll find whether you've been
objective or not."

As he finished, there was a roar of approval, bursts of
laughter, and only a few scowls. Brill felt enormous relief
and even hope that these men would really talk freely. Before the night was out, he would like to go into the homes
of some of them and see and talk to their wives and children, and to the older people who had been associated
with the docks all their lives. He would need to see some
of the ships being worked, hear and see the cranes, watch
the men doing their job. There could be a very good piece
in this, a good, well-rounded piece which might be of help
in the crisis. However, he did not think he would learn
anything about the lumpy objects covered by the thick
sweaters or what was in those baggy, sagging pockets, and
he knew he mustn't inquire.

But he wanted above all things to find out. . . .

That was the first time since he had left Mesurier's
office, three hours or so before, that he completely forgot
Rose.

At the time Malcolm was entering The Docker, Rose

was sitting in front of the dressing table, wearing only her bra and pants and sheer nylons. The bra was a support-from-under kind, very revealing, and usually she wore it with a cocktail dress which was overdaring; she knew that Malcolm didn't like it but she relished the glances that it drew: quick interest from the men, disapproval from their wives.

She had one long dress which she could wear the bra with, too; the dress was more concealing but it was gathered at the neck with two velvet bows, which, if they were too tight, at least hinted—or promised. The trouble with that dress was she could not zip it up at the back herself; Malcolm usually did that, though once or twice Roger had managed.

But it was *the* dress she'd planned to wear for this occasion.

She wanted to be ready when Jack Ledden called, but on the other hand, she was determined to be at her absolute best. And, except for the dress, she was. Make-up was done, perfume was on, everything was ready. Her dark hair had a natural wave and, provided it was well cut, it always looked nice. The tiny diamond earrings drew just enough attention to her small ears. And tonight, perhaps because of her excitement, her eyes were beautiful.

She had to make up her mind. She couldn't wait—

The front doorbell gave its sharp, jarring ring, and now she had no choice; of course she had dallied and dithered until that was inevitable. She slipped into a silk dressing gown, ample in size, and went downstairs, her heart beating very fast. In a moment she would know whether Jack Ledden was really the man she remembered—tall, young, good-looking.

She opened the door, and there he was, holding a corsage of pink and red orchids. He was every bit as good-looking and as tall—and even more distinguished than she had recalled.

"Hal-*lo!*" His voice was deep and reflected the admiration in his blue eyes and the boldness of his nature. "You're just as lovely as I remembered!"

"Flattery, sir, will get you nowhere," she retorted, standing aside. "I'm much nearer ready than I look. Will you come in for a moment?"

"May I?"

It was all a little stilted, a little false; she needed no telling that he had the same brittle feeling as she had. She opened the door of the front room, where Dorothy had stood at the window that afternoon, making no comment about the orchids; the moment for that was not yet. "I won't be two jiffs," she said, and hurried upstairs. Now her heart really was thumping, but she knew exactly what to do. Put on shoes: done! Slip off dressing gown: done! Step into dress so as not to disarrange her hair, slowly, slowly, loving the sensuous feel of the black velvet. The long skirt fitted snugly at the waist but not tightly—she hadn't put on an inch in five years! Arms into the sleeves, which were loose-fitting and wrist length, and hoist the dress over her shoulders—there! She looked at herself in the mirror, and she positively glowed. She put her hands behind her and pulled the zip up by a few inches, at least to show that she'd tried.

Now!

She could call him up, or go down.

The dress was a bit long; until it was fastened all the way up to the neck, she *could* trip over the hem. She hesitated for a moment in delicious uncertainty, then decided that it would be asking for trouble to bring him upstairs. She would go down and get him to fasten the zip and then pop back upstairs for her wrap and bag and gloves.

She moved toward the landing and the stairs.

Jack Ledden was standing at the bottom.

It was almost as if he had been teased by the same temptation; what would she have done if he had come up without being invited?

She did not dwell on the question but beckoned and called, "Come and do me up, will you?"

"Glad to!" He came lightly up the narrow stairs, and from this view in particular he was most striking to look at. She hadn't realized before how far his hair grew back at his forehead, leaving a very pronounced widow's peak. It was shadowy on the landing but bright in the children's bedroom, so she went in there and stood facing him. The gown had dropped off her shoulders; her bosom, lifted by the bra, could not fail to catch his eye.

She saw his gaze drop as she said, "You can see to fasten the zip better from here."

She raised the gown to her shoulders and Ledden slipped behind her. For a moment his fingers fumbled, but suddenly became firm.

He zipped up in a single sweep, and asked, "Isn't there a hook or something?"

"A hook and eye. *You've* done this before!"

"I have a horde of sisters, and a very attractive mother," he told her. His fingers were cool, not cold, on the back of her neck. "There—that's it."

"Thank you." She led the way back onto the landing, adding, "I'll just get my wrap." She went into the bedroom and he went quickly down the stairs. When she followed, only a few moments later, he was out of sight. She held bag and gloves, and wore over her shoulders a lightweight stole of the same velvet as her dress but lined with scarlet satin. Ledden appeared from the front room, carrying the orchids.

"May I pin these on?"

"Do, please," she said

"Have you any particular place you like to wear flowers?"

"Put them wherever you like," she replied.

He selected her waist, on the right side just below the breast, and she felt the pressure of his hands for a moment in rare familiarity. But he was deft and quick. Finished, he stood back and studied her, his appraisal much longer than any she had known for a long, long time.

At last he spoke in a husky voice, saying simply, "You are very beautiful."

"Thank you," she said, her voice also a little husky.

He half turned, opened the door, and went on in the same tone, "I thought so the first moment I saw you—half a year ago."

In a few moments, she was sitting beside him in the back of a chauffeur-driven car. He made no further comment, and she sat in a glow of silence, her heart still beating very fast.

Then suddenly he took and squeezed her hand, and said laughingly, "I don't want to fool you, Rose—I hired the car for the occasion. I don't usually run to a chauffeur. In fact, you could put my M.G. in the trunk of this one! I wanted to use every moment we had without being heart-in-mouth for a taxi, or driving in circles finding a place to park. We're going to the Savoy Grill for dinner. Do you know it?"

"I've been there once or twice," she said, trying to sound casual. "Jack, aren't you being too extravagant?"

He squeezed her hand again, and said lightly, "I want this to be a night to remember! Besides, I didn't have to pay for the tickets!"

"That's true," she agreed, and laughed on a rather nervous note.

That was the first time she had given more than a passing thought to Malcolm since he had left the house and she had realized who was to take her out. Strangely enough, it was from that moment on that she settled down to full enjoyment of the evening. Before then, there had been something clandestine about it, but Malcolm not only knew, he had arranged it. There was nothing at all to prevent her from having a wonderful time.

She put her hand in Jack's, and leaned her head against his shoulder.

7

Vicious Circle

AT THE CROWDED THEATRE there were at least twenty
policemen in plainclothes; there were also two dock employers with their wives and three trades-union officials
and their wives among a host of more than usually distinguished guests. Three press barons were present with
their parties, as well as critics from all the London and
the major provincial newspapers. Among the policemen
was Deputy Commander Alec Hobbs, Gideon's deputy—
and but for her engagement in Edinburgh, Gideon's
youngest daughter would have been with him. As it was,
Hobbs was with the editor of a woman's magazine, who
had been a close friend of his wife's. For Hobbs, a man
who felt a great deal but did not talk much, it was a
strange, compelling, and in some ways nostalgic evening.
He had not seen any of his wife's friends, except on brief
social occasions, since she had died.

He sat watching and listening to *Swan Lake* and enjoy-
ing Natasha, whom he had never seen before. The last time
he had seen the Bolshoi had been here, with his wife. The
woman by his side, Norah Lofting, was tall, beautifully
made-up, and wearing a short evening dress by Hartnell.
Now and again, she glanced at Hobbs, but he was never
looking at her.

Up in the "gods," at the very top, sat a man named
Entwhistle, his knees squeezed against the balcony in

front of him, his eleven-year-old daughter by his side. Both were enthralled. Now and then, Entwhistle stole a glance at the child; she looked radiant. At other times, he would look about him: right and left and over the top to the circle below. To this man, everything had a sense of unreality and at moments he had to pinch himself to realize it was all true.

A dozen times tears stung his eyes.

The tears he fought back were not of hurt or grief, although both were remembered. A few months ago, he had been in Dartmoor Prison, serving life for the murder of his wife, this child's mother. He had been in the very depths of despair and had virtually given up hope, until the child had ventured, by herself, to find her way to Dartmoor.

God! He had nearly lost her!

She had come close to dying on those moors.

But here they were, and here he was, free, "pardoned," and with compensation to come, enough to help him start another life. Very soon they would be on the way to Australia, with his two other children. But for the moment this was all he wanted, for before her death the child's mother had promised that he would take her to see ballet "in a real live theatre." And she had written this to him in a remote part of Africa, where he had been on a construction job, helping to build a bridge between two once-warring, now peaceful nations.

He was free; he was alive again.

His children still lived with their uncle and aunt, virtually their foster parents. There was still so much to do, so many adjustments to make, so many wounds to heal and fears to lull, but tonight here he was, sitting almost directly above Alec Hobbs, who was George Gideon's deputy. And it was Gideon, a hallowed name in Entwhistle's mind, who had given the word to reopen inquiries into the old murder.

Gideon was at his home, waiting for Honiwell, the man who had actually carried out the inquiries which had led to the arrest and confession of the real murderer, who was even now awaiting trial. For many years, Gideon and Honiwell had been little more than casual friends. In the past two years, however, the work at the Yard had thrown them together again in a series of cases in which Gideon had watched the other at work, and realized that he had become a man of deep human understanding and compassion. Before the Entwhistle case, Honiwell had been in charge of two major searches for lost children, each a little girl. Both had been found eventually, murdered. Since that case he had been working exclusively on a case of a very different kind: illegal immigration, particularly of Indians and Pakistanis, into Britain.

This had begun when a row of houses, not fit for human habitation, had collapsed in Notting Hill. That, and the investigation which followed, had revealed a state of affairs which had shocked the most hardened police and social workers: overcrowding of the illegal immigrants, and often their families, in circumstances of sickening congestion and dangerous lack of sanitation—appalling ghetto conditions. The house where the victims lived had been condemned out of hand but there were many others on the borderline. The police had to find answers to these questions:

Who owned the houses?

How much rent was charged?

How many local bylaws and national laws were not simply broken but ignored as if they did not exist?

Who brought the helpless people into the country, and where?

Who brought them to the ghettos?

And who, in the beginning, organized their depar-

ture from their homelands, and organized the ship-
ment of human cargoes and smuggled those cargoes
into Britain?

This inquiry had begun on a great wave of emotional
anger about the disaster, when dozens had died and hundreds had been injured; the public conscience had been
shocked. The public conscience, however, could prove
very fickle unless someone or something was constantly
jogging its memory. This particular cause of anger and
series of crimes had, of course, strong political overtones,
and there had been some hushing up, especially in the
past few months. Now and again, it was revived when a
shipload of people from India or Pakistan was intercepted
within the three-mile limit, or when they had just been
landed. The most notorious instance was when over sixty
men had been found crammed into a cellar and kept there
for forty-eight hours without food or water because the
organizers had believed that the house was being watched
by the police. Finally one of the men involved in the
smuggling had made an anonymous telephone call to the
police.

That had been at a town on the Norfolk coast.

Honiwell, with another senior Superintendent, had the
task of investigating not just that single incident but the
situation throughout the land. Tonight was the first time
he had asked to discuss it with Gideon. Honiwell had
been held up and unable to get to the Yard by a reasonable
hour, and Gideon had eaten at the Yard's canteen, then
had gone home at about eight o'clock. Honiwell was due
at half past.

Gideon went into the small front garden. Kate had left
the hedge and grass trimmed and the narrow flower beds
turned and weeded, and geraniums planted; in a small
garden, she liked to have only one kind of flower each
season and different kinds one year from the next. The
geraniums were red and pale pink, not yet in full bloom.
He stooped down and picked up two pieces of paper from

a chocolate bar and pulled half a dozen weeds so tiny that they were hardly worth worrying about. It was pleasantly warm, and he stood at the wrought-iron gate looking at the front of the house in its new paint and seeing that Kate had put a small concrete bowl just inside the porch, holding two or three geraniums. Where there was a spare corner, she put a flower! Green-fingered Kate Two neighbors passed, each saying, "Good evening, Mr Gideon," but neither lingered. A boy and a girl walked by, arms linked, bodies close. Gideon watched them for a moment, recognized the boy who usually delivered the newspapers, and switched thoughts suddenly to his exasperation that morning and the reason for it.

Was Mesurier's man already at work?

Was Percy Lawless right about the threatened trouble between the dockers and the strikebreakers?

Certainly Sir Giles Rook had been convinced—and, for that matter, so had Gideon—but there was an air of unreality about it all. The need for secrecy troubled him. The fact was that he, Gideon, had joined a conspiracy to evade the normal channels; goodness knows what Yew-Yew Upway would say if he ever found out! But these things were not, of themselves and at this moment, of major importance.

Two things were; not related, yet remarkably alike in some ways.

If there was an organization of Fascists and right-wing extremists called the Strike Breakers, it was one he had never heard of, and for anything of that kind to exist without at least a rumor reaching his ears was quite remarkable. The secret had been very well kept.

So was the secret of the organization of illegal immigrants. Oh, he knew that it existed, but even now the police saw only the tip of the iceberg. It was this which worried him most: that it might be on a very much larger scale than he or anyone else had ever suspected.

And so might the Strike Breakers.

In different ways, each could lead to social distress and

disorder in a disastrous way. If there was a clash tomorrow at any one of the docks and it got out of control, it could delay any hope of peace at the docks indefinitely.

And if there were many overcrowded ghettos still hidden from the local authorities, then there was real danger of epidemics, and grave danger to health, quite apart from the political dangers and the inevitable social unrest.

Gideon, moving into the house, gave a little shudder.

He stopped at the second door on the left, which was at the foot of the staircase, and went into a scene of strange but expected emptiness: painter's dust sheets on the floor, furniture gone, two ladders reaching up to a great hole in the ceiling. In the household this was called Penny's Pothole, and usually brought a smile, but Gideon was not smiling then, for he'd had a new and most disturbing thought.

The Strike Breakers might not stop at just trying to break strikes.

They might attempt to take the law into their own hands in such matters as the immigrants, and shiploads of human beings then could run not simply into the measured obstruction of the law but against the savage antagonism of obsessed men quite capable of using violence.

It was bad enough to think of ships at sea with their holds crammed with men whose one hope and object in life was to get into Britain and become absorbed into the community: it was far worse to think, for instance, that such a ship might be sunk.

He shivered again.

There were, in fact, two shiploads of Pakistanis at sea, one not far off the east coast, one not far off the south. This one, if all went smoothly, would land between Brighton and Eastbourne, guided by a motorboat which would rendezvous with them after dark. The sea was calm. The immigrants, sitting in the hold on long wooden benches or on boxes or on anything which jutted out, were in total darkness. Every now and again, a man prayed in a wailing voice. Every now and again, a man was sick.

The immigrants in the other ship were not so lucky.

They were in a smaller vessel, no bigger than a tug, and had even less room. None was actually sitting, although some could lean against a stanchion or a bulkhead. The hold stank from oil and grease. The sea was choppy and they were never steady for a moment, but went swaying and sprawling, swaying and sprawling.

Many were sick.

One, although the others did not yet know it, was dead.

There were people on the lookout for any vessel which might be carrying immigrants and might seek to land after dark; among them were the coastguards, men on naval and air-force craft, the customs men, and the police at docks and in villages. None was spending full time on this search, but many were keeping a weather eye open.

Another man keeping his eye open for any attempt to smuggle Pakistanis and Indians from Holland or Belgium was a member of the crew of a small Yarmouth fishing trawler. He was a recent member who had put some money into a small fleet; otherwise—since he was from the south—he would never have been accepted by master or men. He was, in fact, one of the committee of a group which called itself the Strike Breakers, and one of several who had infiltrated the ranks of the coastal fishermen. His main task was to find out who helped the immigrants, so that the police could be tipped off, but deep down his one concern was to make sure that as few as possible landed alive.

By the time Matt Honiwell reached Gideon's house, Gideon had recovered from the impact of that ugly thought; it was not completely gone but it did seem to him most unlikely, and it now no longer troubled him. All the same, as he opened the door to Matt and stood aside in a hall just wide enough for two big men to pass, he determined to share the thought; there wasn't a better man to share it with than this big, burly, cuddly-looking man.

8

Honiwell's Fears

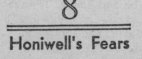

ONE OPENED the front door of Gideon's house onto the passage and to the stairs, half the passage width, beyond. Off the wide section of the passage was the front room. Next to it—with Penny's Pothole in the ceiling—was the dining room, and on the other side was a narrow room, once the kitchen, now a kind of living-*cum*-sewing-*cum*-everyday room, with a television set, books, magazines—a room which was often untidy but, like the rest of the rooms, Kate-clean. Beyond this was the old scullery, made larger and converted—years ago—into a kitchen spacious enough for a big deal-topped table and for the family to eat in.

"Have a look in here," Gideon said, opening the door to the dining room.

Honiwell stepped in, stopped, stared upward, gasped, and after a moment demanded, "Someone drop a bomb on you?" He looked around. "Where's that big dining-room suite? And the sideboard? Where—"

He broke off, went in, and peered up. *"Why?* That's the question? Why make a huge hole in the ceiling?"

"To get into the attic," answered Gideon.

"Now, come off it!"

"All the same, it's true," Gideon assured him, and chuckled. "Did I ever tell you I'd promised Penny that I'd make the attic soundproof so that she could practice her piano day and night, if she wanted to, without disturbing a soul?"

"Yes, but you didn't need to make a hole that size! And in the dining room. What about the bedroom above it?"

"Penny's, nowadays," Gideon answered. "We had some soundproofing and attic-extending specialists in and there were a dozen reasons—mostly water pipes and gas pipes—why they couldn't get up into the loft, or come through the roof. There were also rafter problems for a grand piano and everything she would need up there. But by lowering the ceiling of this room and using Penny's bedroom, it became a practical proposition and they're nearly done. Penny's bedroom will be smaller, the walls are packed with fiberglass and whatever they use for soundproofing. The window's double-glazed. One day next week, they'll hoist the piano up through there and a week after that have the joists and the floorboards back in position—on hinges, so that if we ever wanted the piano down it could be done." When Honiwell made no immediate comment, Gideon went on, "Kate's gone to Pru for a few days until the worst of the noise is over."

"I can't say I blame her," Honiwell said. "But—" He broke off.

"But what?"

"None of my business," Honiwell muttered, "but didn't this cost a fortune?"

"One thousand two hundred pounds."

"Good God! When Penny might—" Honiwell broke off again.

"Get married any day and move to a home of her own. Yes, I know," Gideon said quietly. "Of course she might, but at least—" It was his turn to break off, and Honiwell's to press, but Honiwell simply gulped and made no comment. Gideon turned and led the way into the next room, where there were two huge armchairs on either side of the fireplace; the old iron oven had been taken away and a television set stood where the oven had been, still on the old wrought-iron pedestal. "Cold beer or warm, or would you rather have a brandy?" asked Gideon.

"Cold beer, I think."

Gideon went into the kitchen and brought out two cans of beer and two glasses. He opened the cans and gave one to Honiwell, to pour out and make his own "head." Then they settled down, Gideon facing the door as he always did if he had a chance.

"How's Netta?" he asked.

"Couldn't be better," Honiwell replied. "And Kate?"

"Fine." Gideon raised his glass. "Cheers."

"Cheers."

"Matt," Gideon said, "I imagine the whole of the Yard knows about Penny and Alec Hobbs."

"Have to be deaf not to," Honiwell remarked.

"What's the general reaction?"

"Everyone's for you. Nearly everyone likes Alec Hobbs, so if the match is agreeable to you—and if it wasn't you wouldn't let it develop—good luck to them." Honiwell broke off, drank some of his beer, and then said quietly, "George, we *are* talking as friends, aren't we? I haven't affronted you by calling the Deputy Commander 'Alec'?"

"Good Lord, no!" Gideon was surprised into a broad smile. He knew that Honiwell had been at the Yard long enough to observe all the customs as well as the regulations, and in the office he would not talk of Hobbs except as "Mister" or "Deputy"; nor would he use Gideon's Christian name. But here, yes: they were old friends and closer than many he could recall. The only other man with whom he might have talked freely and with absolute familiarity on any other subject was Hobbs—but not about Penny, not in the circumstances.

"What were you going to say?" Gideon asked.

"What do *you* think about Penny and Hobbs?" asked Honiwell.

"On the whole, I'm more for than against, even though she is fifteen years younger and he's a widower. They've been very good friends for a long time and I think they could be very happy. Neither of them shows any sign of jealousy, each knows the other's career has to be first or near first much of the time. Yes, on the whole I'm glad."

"But you have a doubt," Honiwell said.

"Inevitably, I suppose."

"I daresay," Honiwell conceded. "Are they likely to get married soon?"

"I think Alec would like to," Gideon answered.

"Not Penny?"

"I think she would, on the whole," Gideon replied. "She *had* a lot of doubts and misgivings in case he felt that she should give up her career, but he's reassured her about that." Gideon drank some beer and put the glass on a small table standing inside the fireplace. "So you think I'm crazy to make a soundproof room for Penelope to practice in before they've decided what to do. Isn't that about it?"

"Yes," Honiwell admitted, half smiling. "I think I've a glimmering, but tell me."

"She needs a place to practice," Gideon said. "It has to be a place of her own, where she can go without the slightest fear of causing annoyance or resentment. Alec can give her one, of course—whether they live in a flat or a house, in the heart of London or just outside, he can and will give it to her. But I don't want that to weigh with her when she makes her decision about marrying. I think it would. I think she would hesitate about being at home all the time and exasperating some neighbors and even us. There are times," Gideon said with a smile, "when Kate and I feel we can't stand another arpeggio or another phrase of the same music over and over and over again. This way, she'll make her decision for the right reasons— not the wrong ones."

"That's what I suspected," Honiwell said quietly. "You and Kate—you take the biscuit."

Gideon said, "Kate's the one in this family! More beer?"

"Is there another just as cold?"

"Yes," Gideon said, and went back to the kitchen. Soon he appeared with another straight out of the refrigerator. "This ought to suit you." He opened the can, and went on as it popped and sprayed: "What do you think about the immigration situation, Matt?"

Honiwell took the can, placed it by the empty one, and seemed to hesitate for a long time; then he looked straight into Gideon's eyes and said with great precision, "It scares me stiff."

Until that moment, Gideon had been more relaxed and content than he had been all day, had half forgotten what it was he wanted to talk to Honiwell about. Now disquiet and memory came crowding back, although neither showed in his expression.

"What particular aspects of it?" he asked.

"Three aspects. First, I don't think we yet know the size of the problem and it isn't one we can do on our own. By 'we' I mean the police generally. I've been to the Midlands, the Manchester area, Glasgow, and the northeast, where most of the concentrations of immigrant populations are, outside of London. Our chaps try, but basically it's a matter for the local authorities. Some want to move fast but can't; some are afraid that if they dig too deep they'll find more than they bargained for, and they don't want either the scandal or the possibility of having to do a big rehousing job. And, to be fair, rehousing is a hell of a problem even without complications. I don't think we as the police can or should tackle the major problem. I'd like to suggest we draw up a report, without comment, and give it to the Home Office. And, if I had my way, send a copy to the press."

Gideon, lips pursed, nodded slowly.

"Second, there's the problem of the profiteering landlords," Honiwell went on. "They buy up old property which hasn't yet been condemned, say—swear it's for family use only. They use hundreds of contacts, and cram the illegal immigrants in like cattle. They've even gone as far as arranging to have wholesale supplies of food delivered to the doors, so that some of the poor devils never need get out by daylight. Gradually they are moved to better homes—whenever their families can afford it, that

is. There's another kind of racket going on, too. Some
families unofficially adopt complete strangers, who become boarders, and charge the earth; but at least these
boarders have reasonable food and living conditions.
Eventually all those who get out of the ghettos are found a
place like this and a forged work permit, and they get by.
But while we can't get any accurate figures, there are some
ways of getting approximations. I'd say one immigrant in
ten dies in the ghetto."

Gideon flinched.

"Are you sure?"

"No. But in thirty-seven cases, covering nearly five hundred people, that I have been able to check, it comes out
to more than ten percent, that's why I say ten. It *is* just
possible to check occasionally. Now and again, there's a
deeply conscientious council employee, a rent collector, or
a public health official who dedicates himself to finding
facts. On the whole, we get most help from newspapermen, especially some of the youngsters in the worst areas.
They keep on compiling, putting snippets in the local
newspapers, besieging local councils and M.P.s. Too many
of them come up against a blank wall of 'We don't want
to know.' "

Gideon frowned, but did not interrupt.

"It's absolutely true," Honiwell insisted. "Local newspapers are gossip sheets more than campaigning organs,
and their readers don't really want to know. At least two
have gone out of business because they printed too much
and advertising and circulation dropped. George, this is
an awful problem. It really is."

"Yes," Gideon grunted. "Yes, I can see."

"What it needs is a big nationwide campaign, and what
it still gets is hush-hush and swept under the carpet."

"Are you telling me that the ten percent who don't get
out of these ghettos, as you call them, are killed?"

"They just die."

"But how?"

"Starvation and neglected illness, mostly bronchial. All

of them have visits from Pakistani doctors who are on the lookout for smallpox or typhoid or cholera, and a pretty tight watch is kept on that, although I suspect—" Honiwell gulped and broke off, and while Gideon stared at him as if commanding him to go on, he finished his beer. "George," he said, "I have a bloody awful feeling that if smallpox or cholera is found the patient is allowed to die, and the place where he lived is closely watched. If there are other cases, it is burned. I don't know this for certain, but I do know that several old houses in immigrant quarters have been burned to the ground before the fire brigade could arrive. We're only at the beginning of this business. When Tom Riddell discovered what was going on in that place near Notting Hill, he really started something."

Gideon said, "He certainly did." It passed through his mind that when Detective Superintendent Thomas Riddell had first been assigned to a job concerning immigrants he had wanted to dodge it because of violent color prejudice. Then he had begun to see some of the evidence of overcrowding, victimization, and exploitation, and he had nearly died holding up a house in Notting Hill which, without support from human backs, would have crushed hundreds of immigrants to death.

"George," Honiwell went on, "I know that ninety-five percent of all the immigrants live reasonably and decently —not our way but their way. But even if ninety-nine percent did, and there were two million in Britain altogether, think how many live in hell? Over twenty thousand! And they are continually smuggled in. There's no certainty how many, but several shiploads a week, I would say, each with anything between fifty and a hundred on board. At least one such ship is said to have sunk off the north German coast in the gales last month; certainly a number of bodies were washed up. There was no identification, but finger rings and other adornments suggested the people were Pakistanis. Whoever sends them over from the Continent is absolutely cold-blooded and ruthless. It's an

Interpol job if ever I saw one. I've a written recommendation here." He tapped the briefcase, and then leaned back,
momentarily closing his eyes.

When he opened them again, he said in a hopeless-
sounding voice, "I'm not sure that's the worst, George."

Gideon, already sitting absolutely rigid from tension
born out of Honiwell's manner as well as the story itself,
did not make any comment; simply waited for the other
man to go on

"I believe another ship was deliberately sunk. I think
the holds were battened down, everything that could be
moved was taken off, and she was holed and sent to the
bottom. I'm not sure. I wouldn't say a word about this to
anyone but you. I'm not even sure I ought to tell you, but
I just can't keep it to myself any longer. It's beginning to
prey on my mind."

9

"Old Homer"

THE NAME of the reporter who was at The Docker at the same time as Malcolm Brill was Alan Holmes. Whether that was why he was known throughout dockland and his part of the East End generally as "Old Homer," he did not know, and did not greatly care. He was a tall, pale-faced, thin—in fact, spindly—man in his middle thirties, but he was often taken for being in his early twenties. A mop of dark hair covered his high forehead; huge horn-rimmed glasses concealed the piercing brightness of his eyes. He was something of a caricature of a man to look at, and although he should have been noticeable, few people paid much attention to him. He wrote feature stories on dock-land places and personalities. Within the past three months, for instance, he had featured Willis Murdoch, of the Dock Workers' Union, and Jo Stout, the landlord of The Docker, who had been landlord of the old pub of the same name when it had been pulled down. Dock laborers, sailors, customs men, P.L.A. policemen, captains and mates of ships which come in regularly, especially those from Holland, Belgium, and northern France, appeared in his articles, all of which were well disposed if rather laconic in style.

He felt his greatest triumph was to place a news item with the big newspapers, especially the big "evenings."

One thing certain about Old Homer was that he would never betray a confidence, never write about anything he thought would do harm. The Willis Murdoch article, for instance, had been shown to the dockers' leader before being set in print. Because of this, and because he had been on the same newspaper since he was sixteen—twenty full years—everyone who knew him trusted him. And ignored him; they literally did not notice Old Homer unless they wanted him to put a paragraph in the North Thames group of local newspapers for which he worked; except for Murdoch, none of the others knew that his work sometimes appeared in national newspapers also. The bits of gossip that he obtained were unending in number and variety. Births, deaths, marriages; loves, infidelities, divorces. All of these were good for his column.

He seldom if ever used a pen to take notes; he relied on his phenomenal memory and no doubt this was one important factor in his being accepted by everyone. While his name appeared on all the weekly newspaper articles, it was never on the dailies, but he had a contact at each news desk. He seldom gave a full story, just a tip: "It might be worth having someone at Number Six Pier, Catherine Dock, tonight," or, "There ought to be some fun at the Globe Steps tonight." And this was usually enough to bring a man from Fleet Street.

Tonight he had gone in, as usual, to pick up gossip.

He was reasonably sure in his own mind that there would be a dock strike but that the final demands would be such that they could be met within two or three days. He marveled at the stubbornness and insensibility of both sides. It had become almost a form of duel: honor could not be satisfied until one or the other had drawn blood. He had grown used to this and did not feel for the dockers more than for the employers, but he liked the dockers more because he knew them better.

That night, within a few seconds of stepping inside, he had sensed that something was terribly wrong. Half the men carried weapons of some kind: hammers, bicycle chains, rubber hose, and truncheons; and obviously they were rejoicing in the prospect of using them.

He was horrified, but had not commented or asked a question.

He had heard a few threatening phrases, such as "We'll show 'em!" or, "We'll break their bloody necks!" or, "We'll tear them apart!" But no one had gone into detail, and he could only imagine they were talking about blacklegs, if any men went into work after the strike. Undoubtedly they were preparing for battle, and were boasting to one another.

"The old packing shed just inside the wall," one man said.

"The one with the hole in the roof."

"The flicker's couch!"

"Up lover's lane, you mean!"

They were deciding where they were going to hide their weapons, and were in as raucous and truculent a mood as he had ever known dockers to be, but there was something different tonight: a note of savage triumph.

Suddenly, the main door had opened to admit a stranger.

As suddenly, practically everyone stopped talking. Weapons vanished into pockets, down waistbands, up jerseys; a few were slipped behind chairs, one man put a bicycle chain on his head and covered it with his cap.

The men to whom Old Homer had been talking suddenly seemed to realize that he was not in fact one of them, and a man whispered, "Keep yer trap shut!"

None of the dockers appeared to recognize the man who had just entered, but Holmes recognized him as Malcolm Brill, a fine feature writer and an exceptional reporter. He must be here to cover the pre-strike situation. Alan Holmes watched intently and, after the first shock, began to admire the way Brill handled the situation, so that gradually the mood of the men changed.

One after another they slipped out, including the one who had threatened Brill. Five minutes later, Holmes himself went out and rode on his bicycle away from The Docker, but before long he rested the machine against a wall and walked back. When he was at the dock gates, he saw the men going, in ones and twos, to the old packing shed. It was in fact the spot where, for years, the local whores had worked, and for years two old mattresses had been there, one by each wall; two at a time had been commonplace. The shed had been raided by the police a year ago and everything in it burned and a new padlock put on the door, but tonight the padlock had been opened.

Then there was a lull in the visits to the shed, and Holmes sneaked across the road and found the padlock loose. He looked inside. No one was there, but a pile of weapons showed up in one corner in greater variety than he had realized. There was even an old revolver.

Holmes slipped away and walked back to his bicycle. At every few yards, he looked around to make sure he wasn't followed. This was the first time in twenty years that he had felt scared.

He did not know what to do.

If he knew what they were up to, it would be easy to make up his mind, but if he did the obvious thing and put through an anonymous call to the police, he might do untold harm to men he had lived among all his life.

Was there to be a gang fight?

Was there a group of dockers who wanted to stay inside the dock walls and so intensify the strike?

Who would know the answers? He asked himself time and time again who would *know*. Murdoch, of course, but he wouldn't talk. Everyone who had been in The Docker knew, obviously, but they wouldn't breathe a word. There were a few men in the district who might know and whose tongues could be loosened by a pound or two, but if he approached the wrong man it could lead to disaster.

A loner by nature and by training, he was urgently in need of someone to talk to. Supposing he could find Brill? He went across to the pub again. It was nearly empty, and Jo Stout was polishing glasses behind the bar.

"The little chap?" bald-headed Jo asked. "He went off with Willis."

Holmes nodded his thanks and went out as two Indians or Pakistanis entered the pub, followed by two Jamaicans. He straddled his bicycle again and made a tour of the outside dockgate area but saw no one. Next, he went inside the docks—he was known to everyone and was never refused entry—wondering if he could catch up with Brill at one of the ships. The clanking and the squealing of cranes and derricks was unending. Ship after ship showed in floodlights and men were silhouetted against the brightness, but none was Brill or Murdoch. It was anybody's guess where they had gone; to another pub, possibly, or to a lodge meeting, or a union meeting: Murdoch knew how to use the press to fullest advantage. Disconsolate and also very troubled, Holmes left the dock. There was no desperate urgency; obviously the weapons were not going to be used until tomorrow—

At the dock gates, of course!

Suddenly, his mood changed. Still on his bicycle, he rode to three different dock gates, using short cuts which comparatively few people knew about. He had a vivid picture of each one in his mind, and of the equivalent to the old shed just inside Gate 1. At the first, there was a broken-down railway carriage, once used for the same purpose as the shed. He leaned his bicycle against it and climbed in, shining his torch beneath the once-padded, now skeletal seats.

Here were dozens more weapons, only partly covered with old sacks.

He cycled, heart beating fast, to Gate 3, where the most likely hiding place was a cycle shed close to a dilapidated warehouse just outside the huge wooden gates. The weapons here were in boxes with canvas thrown over them; and among them were two knives and an old prison flail. He left, his heart thumping, and went on to three more gates. At each, he found a store of weapons. Obviously the men planned to come to work tomorrow without any weapons, to make sure they weren't taken away, and then later fetch them from the hiding places. Tonight there was no danger of the weapons being found on their persons as no alarm was on.

By the time he had finished, it was nearly nine o'clock.

He was puzzled, alarmed, and exasperatingly hungry, and he did not know what to do. Willis Murdoch must know about these weapon stocks, since he had been at The Docker when talk had been so free, and Willis wasn't a man to incite violence. At any other time, Holmes would have gone to see Willis, to warn him.

They *were* going to make trouble at the dock gates, but who were they going to fight? It didn't make sense. He was nearer The Docker than any other pub when he felt he couldn't go without food any longer; the choice lay between hot pies at the bar, washed down with beer, or hot pies at a small, mucky café, washed down by lukewarm tea or coffee. He could not face the café and went to the pub. More customers were present now, including half a dozen women—more truly girls—playing darts in a corner. The pie oven was nearly empty and Jo Stout was putting some cold ones inside.

"Couple of hot ones for me, Jo?" asked Old Homer.

"Two of the best," Jo assured him, and took a couple out with his fingers, then wrung his hand exaggeratedly and blew on his fingers. "I should let them cool, Homer, if I was you." He paused, then added, "Four bob—with half a bitter, five and a half. Haven't got the odd penny, have you?"

Old Homer gave him the exact money and went to a small table with his pies and tankard. The hot pies oozed fat, and a flavor all too rare these days. He enjoyed the food and the beer and the relaxation, only just beginning to realize how tired he had been after his burst of cycling. He was halfway through the second pie when the door opened and Willis Murdoch came in with Malcolm Brill.

Brill's the man I want to talk to! Homer decided. And he told himself that it was only a question of getting out first, waiting, and following the man from the *Daily News* Obviously the newcomers would be here for a while so he did not have to hurry, and he did not relish the thought of standing about outside for too long. But after ten minutes he went out, passing Murdoch, who appeared studiously to avoid him. He went around to the side, where there was a small latrine with a faint light outside the entrance, and came out a few minutes afterward. After taking three steps, he was suddenly, frighteningly, aware of men on either side of him. Before he could turn, he felt a savage blow on the back of his head, and on the instant he lost consciousness.

Malcolm Brill left The Docker, with Willis Murdoch, at ten o'clock. Murdoch offered to drive him to Fleet Street but was obviously tired, and Brill decided to catch a bus which would not only take him to Ludgate Circus and the north end of Fleet Street, but would give him time to think. And he needed to think. Willis went off and Brill looked about for Old Homer—or Alan Holmes, as he knew him—half expecting the stringer to be waiting for him. Perhaps Murdoch had scared him off. Brill was not sorry. He had learned a great deal and seen a great deal, and preferred to put his own interpretation on it all. As he settled down in a seat on the top deck, he smiled faintly; he wasn't even sure that the paper would come out tomorrow.

The bus stopped opposite some hoardings, and on them was a double-crown poster, reading:

THE COVENT GARDEN THEATRE
ANNOUNCES
A FULL SEASON OF
14 NIGHTS
OF THE
BOLSHOI BALLET
FROM MOSCOW

He wondered how Rose was getting on, but he didn't think about her for long. The whole of the situation at the docks fascinated him. Of the impending trouble he had no doubt at all.

Rose's hand was in Jack Ledden's. She was aware of the slight pressure of his leg from knee to thigh. She was more acutely conscious of him than of the astounding virtuosity of the ballet dancers. She was thinking how tired she was of the boredom of her marriage, what a mistake it had been. Her heart hadn't raced like this for years. Even the touch of his fingers excited her, so cool on her arm.

Carol Entwhistle's eyes were huge and glowing. She simply could not take her eyes off the stage. She had withdrawn her hand from her father's and was leaning forward, so still that she hardly seemed to be breathing.

Alec Hobbs slowly became very much aware of the fact that Norah Lofting was next to him, not Penelope. It was the first time he had been out on such an occasion without Penelope for nearly two years. Then his attention was drawn away from the stage, from the hushed audience, from Norah, until he could "see" and think only about Penelope. The last vestige of doubt as to how he felt about her and how much he wanted to marry her was gone.

The master of the S.S *Breem,* at sea off the east coast of Britain with its hatches battened down, picked out the light of the motorboat with which he had a rendezvous. The wind was stronger and the sea choppy, but he did not give a thought to the men down below, although two more were close to death in the stinking hold. Soon he was able to pick up the signals, and they were very positive: *"Too dangerous tonight. Same place same time tomorrow night."*

The crew of a small fishing vessel, coming home late because of a big catch, saw the signals.

The master of the S.S. *Desdemona,* in calmer seas,

scanned the cliffs near Beachy Head on the south coast for a signal. With him on the bridge was a younger man, also watching.

The master, cap askew, trousers tight, all-weather jacket flapping, said in a taut voice, "If we don't get in tonight, half those poor devils below will be too weak to walk."

The other made no comment, and they stood together in the stillness with the sea lapping as they lay at anchor, until suddenly a light flashed three times in quick succession.

"There it is!" cried the master. "Thank God for that!"

Holmes came to with a splitting headache, and feeling very hot. Gradually he realized that he was rolled up in a sleeping bag which was tied around at his shoulders, waist, and ankles. Only his head was clear. But he could not call for help any more than he could move, because of adhesive tape stuck over his mouth.

His rather plump, rather pretty, very blond wife, Harriet, in their three-bedroom house in Bethnal Green, switched off the television, and bustled about with the late-night chores. She hoped Alan would be home before she went to bed, but it would neither surprise nor worry her if he were not. Sooner or later he would be here; sooner or later he would be banging away on his old typewriter, which she sometimes believed he loved more than he loved her or their three children. In a funny way, she loved it, too. That was why she called the battered machine Old Homer.

Gideon sat up late, poring over the facts and figures which Honiwell had left for him. He was absorbed in them, not far from obsessed. It was one of the few nights when he thought of one problem only, oblivious of the crime taking place all over London: the break-ins, the burglaries, the rapes, the vice in all its forms, the telephone coin boxes being forced open, the smuggling, the passing of forbidden drugs, the fixes, the plotting—the vast array of what could loosely be called the "professional" crimes for which the police were on the watch. Squad cars would be at the ready, other cars patrolling, men on their beat talking to Information, which might be miles away. London's criminals and London's police were locked in their nightly, silent struggle.

Dozens of "personal" crimes were being committed, too, or being thought about or planned. The wife-beatings, the child-bashings, the stealing from gas and electricity meters, perhaps, the murders by man or wife or lover. The petty pilfering and the major thefts, the embezzlements, the frauds—every crime in the calendar was being committed, planned, or plotted, and the police would know nothing about any of them until they had been reported.

What they needed were X-ray eyes!

But Gideon still concentrated on that one major problem: illegal immigration and its consequences. It wasn't until his telephone rang, just before midnight, that he was jerked out of the absorption; and it wasn't until the man at the other end said "This is Charles Mesurier" that he switched his thoughts to the troubles at the docks, his major preoccupation earlier in the day.

"Two things, Commander," Mesurier said, in his measured way. "The newspaper strike is off, at least for the time being. But I would very much like to talk to you about the situation at the docks, and I have the man I assigned to the job with me. May we come and see you, at once?"

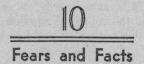

10

Fears and Facts

GIDEON PUT OUT whisky and brandy and some biscuits, and plugged in a percolator for coffee. The front room was crowded with furniture from the dining room, so he would have to talk to the newspapermen in the room where he had seen Honiwell. He wished, vaguely, that he could have used the best room but it did not trouble him as it would have troubled Kate. He kept pondering the way Mesurier had spoken; the very fact that he wanted to come was a measure of the urgency he felt, but that "at once," spoken in his quiet deliberate way, lingered in Gideon's mind. It was quarter past twelve when the front doorbell rang and he went to let them in. Before he could speak, the smaller of the two men, a stranger to Gideon, spoke in a low-pitched voice which also carried a sense of urgency.

"I don't think we were followed, but I'd like to make sure."

Instead of asking "By whom?" or raising any kind of difficulty, Gideon said, "We can soon find out without standing on the doorstep." He let them in, and ushered them toward the living room, then picked up a telephone, which was by the kitchen door, dialed the Yard's information office, and said, "Commander Gideon . . . It's just possible that someone is taking too much interest in my home. Have it checked, will you, and call me back?" He rang off on the man's "Right, sir," and followed the two men into the living room. "It's been known to happen," he remarked. "Whom do you expect—militant dockers or others?"

"Both," the small man answered.

"Commander, I'm sure Mr. Brill would not raise any alarm without feeling justified. Have you met before? . . . Malcolm Brill, Commander Gideon."

They shook hands.

Gideon motioned them to chairs, found that both preferred coffee, heard a little about the temporary settlement of the strike in Fleet Street, recalled some of Brill's searching articles, and even remembered his photograph; but the man was smaller than he had expected and not at all impressive to look at. He seemed so young, with his pale green eyes, his pallid face smeared thick with freckles, and his fair hair slicked over his big, bumpy head. Gideon poured out coffee and sat in an old rocking chair. Hardly had he steadied the chair than the telephone rang. He put his coffee on the table and went to the phone.

"Gideon . . . Are you sure? . . . Good, thanks." He rang off, saying as he moved back to his chair, "You don't appear to have had company when you arrived and certainly no one's loitering now."

"Good," said Mesurier, with obvious relief. In this light, his brown eyes and lean face seemed almost baleful.

"I thought I was followed when I got off a bus from the docks and walked to Mr. Mesurier's place," Brill explained. "I spent the evening in the dock area, much of the time with Willis Murdoch, and some of the dockers resented it."

"Did you find out about the Strike Breakers?" asked Gideon.

"Strike Breakers?" Brill echoed, looking puzzled.

"I didn't tell him anything you'd told me," Mesurier said. "I wanted him to draw his own conclusions."

"Strike Breakers!" breathed Brill. "That would explain it."

"Explain what?" demanded Gideon.

"I pretended not to notice, but a lot of the men at The Docker and other places I went to were carrying weapons," Brill answered. "They hid them when I appeared but they had them all right, from rubber hose to knuckle-dusters and bicycle chains to hammers. It was as if they were getting ready for a real shindig, not a scrap where they'd simply use their hooks. There was a lot of resentment at my being there. Murdoch took me to some private homes and to one where a committee was at work, and of course my ostensible interest was in the strike. But there was something much more than strike action on their minds. What *is* this about the Strike Breakers?"

Gideon told him briefly, and his impression of Malcolm Brill rose sharply. The man saw all the implications quickly, and obviously was deeply concerned.

When Gideon had finished, Brill said to Mesurier, "Then I think I'm right not to do that piece for tomorrow."

"So do I," the news editor agreed, and added by way of explanation to Gideon, "Brill feels that the situation at the docks is so delicate that anything he writes could do more harm than good."

"I hope all the press thinks that way."

"They won't," said Mesurier. "The *Mail* and the *Express* say the time has come for a showdown, and they would back the dock employers to the limit. I'm going to do an editorial asking both sides to have a four-week cooling-off period, but—" He broke off, with a thin-lipped smile. "Well, this isn't anything to worry you with, Commander."

"Don't be too sure," Gideon said. "Apart from knowing that a strike will be another blow to our export trade, if trouble's brewing we need to have a lot of men at the ready."

"And the recorded crime rate will go up," Brill remarked dryly.

"Do you agree?" Mesurier asked Gideon.

"When wages and money are short, there are always people on the fringe who add to the pilfering and petty thieving," Gideon said. "But I'm not worried about that. There could be—well, you know the dangers as well as I do. The question is, how can we sidetrack the worst?" He rocked a little, frowning, and at last went on: "Will you fix that paragraph in a late edition, Mr. Mesurier?"

"Yes."

"Will you send me a copy of it, at the office, in the morning?"

"Yes."

"Then we'll take it from there," Gideon said, and added, "I'm very grateful."

Mesurier spread his hands.

"As I said this afternoon, I'll be glad to help at any time. Have you been able to give much thought to the dock-strike situation, Commander?"

"Not enough," Gideon admitted.

"No doubt that's true of all of us," Mesurier said. He linked his hands together, rather as if in prayer, and went on, "If there is an attempt to cause trouble tomorrow, and if you are able to prevent it from developing, it's just conceivable that the two sides in the dock dispute will find common cause. Then both sides have to thank you. I've been wondering if there is anything at all you or the police could do to get them talking again."

Gideon said heavily, "I can't imagine the Home Secretary agreeing we should even try."

"I suppose not," Mesurier agreed moodily. "All the same—" He stared over the tips of his fingers at Gideon. "Will you consider it?"

"I'll let it drift through my mind," Gideon promised, and added, with a curious kind of laugh, "I wouldn't let fear of the consequences stop me if I thought there were half a chance. How did you avert your strike in Fleet Street?"

Brill said, out of the blue, "Mr. Mesurier worked himself into the ground to get a postponement. At least we've a month to play with." After a moment's pause, the little man suddenly banged a clenched fist into the palm of his hand, and his eyes blazed, his whole face seeming to catch alight. "Why the devil can't both sides see that it's in their own interest to find the answers? Why do they have to behave like enemies? I spent the evening with Willis Murdoch, and that man believes absolutely in what he's doing. He's not a troublemaker or a Commie; he just wants the best terms he can get for his men, but he never looks at the industry as a whole He never seems to realize that he can't get the best terms if the docks aren't flourishing. And the Dock Employers' Federation people are the same. They can only get the best profit and the best job if they've a satisfied labor force, but they seem to see organized labor as a mortal enemy. Why can't they get around the table to work out the best way to get the most for everybody? Why do they *have* to be enemies?"

The last word seemed to ring and echo about the room. Enemies—enemies—enemies!

Gideon had a swift understanding of how this man felt, what put such understanding and compassion into his articles. And Mesurier, now looking at the feature writer over the tips of his fingers, was smiling in obvious approval.

He said quietly, "They don't have to be. Traditionally they are. And it's the same with most of industry." He parted his hands and began to get up. "I wanted to be quite sure you knew that the dockers were ready for the Strike Breakers, Commander. Good luck for tomorrow." He rose to his full height as Brill stood up more slowly. Brill was obviously still carried away by his own rhetoric and passion, and he drew his hand across his forehead, muttering, "People are such fools! Even the best of them." Then he seemed to change his attitude, actually seemed to shrink as he added, "I'm sorry, Commander. I shouldn't let myself go."

Gideon said quietly, "Until you rang, I had been letting myself go about a different situation altogether. So had one of my senior officers."

"On what subject?" Mesurier asked.

"Illegal immigrants and Rachmanism among land-lords," said Gideon. "Can this be off the record?"

"Yes," Mesurier promised.

"Yes," echoed Brill. "Until you release it."

"There's a rumor that a shipload of immigrants went down with all on board a few weeks ago. There are at least two shiploads off the coast at this moment, waiting to slip past the coastguards and the police. The whole situation wants taking up by a newspaper who will really get behind it." His expression seemed to ask Mesurier, "How about you?"

Brill raised his arms and dropped them helplessly to his sides.

Mesurier said, "Not the *Daily News,* I'm afraid. We've cried 'wolf' on the subject far too often. You need one of the bigger, mass-circulation papers, but the trouble is that the political overtones are such that they'd fight shy of it." His eyelids drooped; Gideon was slowly beginning to realize that this was a mannerism which indicated that he was concentrating very hard. "How official is this?"

"The lost ship, strictly—"

"Off the record, no doubt! I would tell any big-circulation paper, though. It might slip onto the record—the need for a major national campaign to draw attention to the landlord racketeering and the extent of the illegal immigration. Would you like to talk to one of the owners who could help if he would?"

"Very much," Gideon said.

"I'm seeing them all tomorrow at eleven o'clock," Mesurier said. "I'll fly a kite or two, Commander."

Gideon had a feeling that he almost said, "George."

Brill, very quiet after his outburst, said "Good night," and followed Mesurier out of the room and the house. Gideon saw them to Mesurier's car, an old vintage Bentley, and went back as a church clock not far away struck one.

Mesurier, who lived in a flat near St. Paul's, drove Brill home and left him, and Brill, who had sat silent, went along to the front door. He was, in fact, extremely thoughtful—half vexed with himself for his outburst, half pleased because Gideon had reacted at least as well as Mesurier. And there was no doubt at all that Gideon was on the side of the angels as far as he, Brill, was concerned. Any man was who believed that two sides should work together, not in conflict. His thoughts ranged over all that had happened that night, and his two concerns were the threatened conflict and the man he knew as Old Homer. He would have liked to talk with the other newspaperman.

He went in, very quietly—a habit developed so as not to wake the children; and tonight out of concern for Rose. It was half past one, and she would have been home an hour or more ago. As only a faint landing light was on, he knew she had gone to bed. He went to the downstairs lavatory so as to avoid running water upstairs, where it could be very noisy, and then went upstairs with hardly a sound.

Then he saw that the main bedroom door, as well as the children's doors, was wide open; he knew that when Rose went to bed on her own, she made a point of closing the door. He went in, puzzled, and made sure she wasn't in bed. He switched on the light and saw the odds and ends lying about; toiletries, two bras, a pair of dress shoes obviously rejected for the night; most certainly she hadn't been back.

But it was after half past one. Where was she?

"Jack," Rose said, nibbling at Ledden's ear, "I must go. It's half past one. You must help me dress and do me up at the back again."

"Every time I undo you," Jack Ledden said, "I shall oblige by doing you up again. But not yet. Not just yet."

Quite suddenly, he was upon her—insatiable.

I wish he would come now, Old Homer's wife thought drowsily. It must be nearly two o'clock.

Soon, however, she slept.

Her husband lay in a stupor between consciousness and unconsciousness, between sleeping and waking, in the packing shed only a short distance from the dock gate.

Brill lay awake, hardly able to think clearly, only able to fear. Every now and again, he got off the wide double bed and went to the window, watching for a few moments, but there was no sign of Rose. At three o'clock, he was on the point of calling the police, or Ledden, or even Maisie; he had to do something—he could not believe that Rose would stay out as late as this deliberately; there must have been an accident The police was a nonsense thought, but the need to talk to someone, to ask about Rose, was overwhelming; and suddenly he went downstairs into the little room where he worked, looked Ledden's number up in the directory, and stood with his finger hovering over the dialing circle.

It was crazy.

But he *must* find out!

If there had been an accident—

He dialed, shivering as he did so from fatigue or from anxiety or from some secret fear. *Brrr-brrr Brrr-brrr.* The ringing sound went on and on until he banged the receiver down, and stood by it, trembling

Where was she?

Had there been an accident?

He couldn't simply wait His own news desk might have some information, or at least would be able to get some quickly He—

A car sounded outside, slowing down.

He turned toward the passage door, listening, then went into the front room, not turning on the light He heard the engine idling; then suddenly it stopped The silence seemed absolute. No door slammed, no footsteps sounded. He went to the window, which was bay-shaped so that one could look in both directions along the street No one was toward the right, but a small car was double-parked a few yards along on the left. The rear lights seemed vivid in the near darkness.

As his eyes grew accustomed to the effect of the car lights, in the dim street, he saw two heads in the car, close together His mouth seemed to go dry His body became as of stone. But he made himself move at last, and went upstairs to the main bedroom, his and Rose's This also was at the front and had a bay He moved to the left side. Now he could see the couple, in each other's arms; he saw the man kissing and caressing the woman, whose hair was dark, like Rose's. He knew that this was Rose and Ledden but refused to admit it. He hated himself for watching but could not make himself turn away

He drew in a hissing breath.

That man's *hands*—

At last, the woman moved She opened the door and got out. She was Rose The man got out the other side; he was Ledden. Rose, head tilted back, was wearing her favorite black dress. Oh, dear God! Ledden came around the car and slid his arms beneath hers from behind, and held her. They were drunk with love. He had never seen Rose more beautiful. Never.

God!

He would like to cut Ledden's hands off!

Homecomings

Rose said, whispering, "You must let me go."

"Never."

"But you must!"

"Never and never and never!"

"Jack, *please*."

"When will you see me again?"

"I—I don't know when."

"*When?*"

"Soon—soon."

"Tomorrow? That's today, now."

"If—if I can "

"You must swear to it or I won't let you go "

"All right," she whispered. "I swear "

"Seal it with a kiss "

"Jack—"

"With a *kiss!*"

She leaned her head back against his shoulder. His hands were upon her bosom, and slowly his lips were upon hers; insatiable in every way Even now she felt desire stirring, and his hands moved, and she almost sobbed.

"Jack, please."

"Tomorrow."

"Yes, tomorrow."

"And remember, that means today."

"I—I'll remember."

"Walk straight to the front door," he said. "Let yourself

in. When you've gone in and closed the door, I'll drive
off."

"All right."

"And—don't look round."

"All right."

"Go," he urged.

She half expected him to draw her back, but he did not.
She walked away from him, feeling more than a little
dizzy, and faltered at the curb.

Malcolm saw her He stood like a block of ice—
watching.

Ledden made no move.

Rose climbed the low step and approached the door,
making very little sound. Suddenly, she disappeared from
her husband's line of vision. She must be on the porch. He
heard her key. He heard the door open. Ledden watched
every movement—tall, dark, handsome, dashing Jack
Ledden. The door closed Ledden turned on the instant
and took the wheel of his car, an old-fashioned M.G.,
which started with a surprisingly low-pitched hum The
car moved off. There was no footstep on the stairs.

"Oh, God," breathed Malcolm Brill, "don't let me kill
her."

He heard nothing

But he could imagine her in the other man's arms.

My God, if the man were here he would break his
neck!

He—he could kill her. Kill his Rose.

Oh, God, dear God, dear God. Don't let me.

There she was! On the stairs. Here she came. She was
halfway, for a stair creaked on a familiar note. In a moment she would be here. He began to shiver. He knew
what he wanted to do. *Wanted to do*. He wanted to place
his hands around her white throat, *his* hands, and squeeze
—and squeeze.

Oh, God, don't let me kill her.

She was on the landing; there was another creak, familiar as the one lower down. He could not bear to set his

eyes upon her. If he saw her, he would leap upon her; if he touched her—*God!* He was quivering violently. He was hot and he was cold. Hot, cold.

She went past to the bathroom.

He began to sweat.

He would do this when he was late: pass the bedroom, undress in the bathroom, come in here, and slip into bed, trying not to disturb her. He had once stayed downstairs and slept on the couch and she had reproved him playfully.

"I don't mind you waking me up."

"But I hate disturbing you."

"It makes me realize I'm married."

He was sweating; his teeth were clenched; he was shivering, hot and cold, hot and cold. Water ran in the bathroom, not the flush but from the taps. He moved slowly toward the door. He knew what he must do; it was as if his prayers had been answered, and he was being saved from killing her. He knew that if he saw her he would lose his self-control. He must not see or touch her. He picked up his dressing gown from the end of the bed and went out of the bedroom. The bathroom door was ajar, light streamed out in a narrow strip. The squeak of the floorboards was drowned, even those on the stairs. He went into the front room, and lowered himself slowly onto the arm of the couch. Then he began to shake as if his whole body were possessed. He could not stop his teeth from chattering, his hands and feet from quivering.

All thought vanished.

There were sounds and noises in his head but no thoughts at all.

He heard nothing from upstairs. After a while, he quietened. She did not come down. He went to a corner cupboard and took out a bottle of brandy, sipped from the bottle, and soon began to feel more in control of himself. He thought he heard the bed creak, feared she would come down, but there was no further sound on the landing or the stairs.

"He's still out," Rose breathed to herself. "He's even later than I am!"

And then she thought, I could have stayed another half-hour with Jack.

Entwhistle could not sleep that night for sheer joy. Every moment at the ballet had been joy; and Carol's delight almost unbelievable. She was in her usual bed; he was sleeping on a convertible sofa in the front room of the little modern house where his brother and sister lived. He got up, dressed, and went out the back door, making no sound at all. He had learned to move with stealth.

He remembered what he had remembered in agony a thousand times.

He remembered going out one night because he could not rest at his home. He had gone out for peace and the quiet of his soul, and come back—and found his wife dead.

In a daze, in horror, in disbelief, he had gone out again and walked the streets, and because of this had later been arrested and charged and convicted of her murder. Now he was out in the streets walking. Alone, without fear or horror or dread. He had a peace in his heart which he had never expected to know again. There were problems and difficulties ahead and some would be hard, but he was back with his children, and the loss of his wife no longer hurt.

The first problem would be what to do about the children.

Should he try to make a home for them himself, in Australia?

Or should he see if his brother and sister, foster parents for so long, would really be happy if they were to stay? He could pay for their upkeep now, get a job and take the financial burden away; he had no doubt about that. Nor had he any doubt that with his newfound calmness he could face any situation. His children knew now that he had not killed their mother, and Carol loved him.

He walked for half an hour.

He passed two policemen at one corner, and was passed at another corner by a small car carrying a reporter and a photographer to the scene of a bank robbery only a mile away. Their world, so much part of his, was also so far away from it. He went back to the house and let himself in quietly, calmly, and went to bed.

This time, he slept.

Gideon woke to his alarm clock at quarter to eight, hurried down to find the newspapers in the letter box, made some tea and scanned the headlines, then had a quick bath and drove to the Yard, arriving there at quarter to nine. He saw the pile of reports on his desk, showing that Hobbs had been busy. He skimmed them all. None was important enough to make him want to see the Superintendent in charge. He rang for Alec Hobbs, who came in from the adjoining room at once. Hobbs was a man of barely medium height, compact, with close-fitting clothes. He had a curious kind of elegance—or, Gideon wondered, was it fastidiousness? Of all the men at the Yard, Gideon had come to like, respect, and trust him more than any, although Gideon was London Elementary School and thereafter self-taught, while Hobbs came of a wealthy and old family, had been to Repton and King's, Cambridge. His dark hair had a suspicion of a wave; his dark gray eyes, somber for so long during the illness and eventual death of his wife, could sparkle as brightly as Penelope's. This morning he wore a suit of light-weight medium gray worsted; Savile Row-tailored.

"Good morning, Alec."

"Good morning, sir."

"How was the ballet?"

"Brilliant," Hobbs replied. "It was a thousand pities Penny missed it."

"There'll be others."

"None quite like that. Natasha is superb." Hobbs, standing now by the side of Gideon's big, flat-topped desk,

with the trays marked "In," "Out," "Pending," "Urgent,"
was obviously assessing Gideon's mood. He smiled faintly
as he went on: "I somehow don't think the Bolshoi Ballet
is on your mind!"

"No," Gideon said. "Two things are, Alec. Sit down."
He told Hobbs what he could of the dockers' strike and
the Strike Breakers, and paused for a reaction. It wasn't
long in coming.

"The moment the news breaks, you'll tell Yew-Yew, I
suppose."

"Yes. But I won't tell him I had foreknowledge."

"No," Hobbs conceded. "Of course, he could still rush
in and cause a lot of trouble thinking he's really staving it
off."

"So," Gideon said.

"It might be—" Hobbs began, and then smiled. "You're
a step ahead, no doubt."

"Of what?"

"The one thing which could keep Yew-Yew from over-
doing it would be a direct warning from the Commissioner," Hobbs said.

Very slowly, Gideon said, "Yes." A variety of thoughts
passed through his mind, including the fact that Hobbs
was right and the time might have to come for someone
to approach the Commissioner, the top official of the
Metropolitan Police. Hobbs was being groomed for the
Assistant Commissionership of the C.I.D., and when he
was commissioned he, not Gideon, would be the man to
go direct to the Commissioner. *Was* this as good a time
as any to start? "Yes," he repeated more crisply. "Will you
get in touch with him?"

Hobbs, for once, looked startled, and there was a noticeable pause before he said, "If that's what you would
like—of course."

"Keep me posted," Gideon said, and went on in the
same breath, so that the two things appeared to be connected, "I've plenty on my hands over the immigration
problems. I spent an hour with Honiwell last night." He

explained what Honiwell had told him, watching Hobbs's dark eyes all the time. "I'd like to concentrate on that problem for a while, Alec. It worries me."

Hobbs said slowly, "That I can well understand. But—" His voice trailed off.

"But what?"

Hobbs still hesitated. He seemed in a way to have withdrawn within himself, to be further away from Gideon, even aloof; and this was how he had seemed to Gideon when they had first started to get to know each other. At that time, Gideon had been suspicious of it; now he knew that Hobbs was simply being very cautious, not of offending but of being right in what he said. There was an admixture of deference, too. Gideon did not press him again.

"George," Hobbs said, "it's not really a job for us."

"You mean it's a job for the Home Secretary and the local as well as the Whitehall government?"

"That and more," replied Hobbs. "If we do more than we should, we could easily be reprimanded, and afterwards it might be difficult to do even as much as we should. There's the thinnest of dividing lines between what is our job and what is the Ministry's."

"Yes," Gideon agreed. "That's why—" He hesitated.

Hobbs did not press, either, but stood very still, very intent. They made a remarkable contrast: Gideon so much bigger and more massive, the other so compact. Each in a different way gave an impression of power under complete control.

"That's why I asked Mesurier last night if he'd take the whole thing up and make a public outcry," Gideon remarked.

"Try to arouse the public conscience, you mean?"

How well he understood Gideon! "Yes, that's exactly what I mean."

"Ten to one he declined with thanks," Hobbs said. He went on as if he were thinking aloud: "Now, if we could get one of the popular papers to take it up—the *Mirror* or the *Express,* for instance—" Hobbs broke off, and looked startled, for Gideon burst out laughing, and after a moment his own lips curved in amusement.

Gideon waved a hand.

"That was exactly what Mesurier suggested," he said, "and with much the same look on his face!" He sobered quickly, and added, "He wasn't optimistic but said he would sound some of the newspaper owners out."

"Then he must think there's a faint chance," Hobbs remarked. "Whether we ought to talk to any prospects, I really don't know. If anyone does, it must be you, sir. Yes," he added in a decisive voice when Gideon waved his hand in disclaimer. "I don't know what it is about you, but you come nearer to bridging the gap between the police and the press than anyone in London." When Gideon made no comment, Hobbs went on, wholly serious although in a musing voice: "I've never really understood the relationship, and I doubt if you do. You simply have a sense of timing and a knowledge of your man. It's a kind of armed peace. When we're not complaining bitterly about them, they're complaining we never give them a story in time and never ask for their help until it's too late. *Do* you know why we're always suspicious of each other?"

Gideon, surprised by the question and by what amounted to an outburst from Hobbs, made no attempt to answer quickly and, in fact, was considering several different aspects of the question when there was a tap at the door and a messenger came in. He carried a large, loosely packed envelope, addressed in a bold hand, in deep black ink: *"Commander George Gideon, Scotland Yard. Urgent."*

This was the newspaper with the inspired "leak."

12

Clash

GIDEON TORE OPEN the envelope and pulled out three copies of the same newspaper, handed one to Hobbs, and scanned the stop-press column on the front page There in large type was the statement:

> ### CLASH AT DOCKS?
> Indications at several London docks are that a clash may be expected between dock workers at their dock-gate strike meeting at noon today and a right-wing organisation called the Strike Breakers In later editions see story on Page 1.

Hobbs looked up as Gideon did; and as their eyes met, Gideon's telephone rang.

Gideon moved around toward it, saying, "Tell the Commissioner at once, Alec I'll take one of these to Upway." He lifted the telephone. "Gideon "

Hobbs was already on his way back to his own office. Gideon was reading the "leak" again.

"Seen it?" The voice was Percy Lawless's.

"Just this moment " Gideon could not keep the satisfaction out of his voice

"Nice work, George!"

"I hope so. I'm going to call Upway right away."

"Best of British luck! I won't keep you." Lawless rang off as Gideon put his receiver down and then dialed Upway's number on the internal telephone. He could almost see the elation on Lawless's face; he could picture Malcolm Brill's face, too, and Mesurier's.

A man answered. "Commander Upway's office."

"Gideon," grunted Gideon. "Is Mr. Upway in?"

"Well, sir, if it's urgent—"

"Put him on the line!" roared Gideon.

There was a moment's pause, and voices sounded in the background before Upway spoke. He had a rather nasal but well-controlled voice which always sounded faintly artificial. At this moment, it seemed to smack of resentment, too.

"This is Commander Upway. I understand Commander Gideon wishes to speak to me."

Gideon asked, without preamble, "Have you seen the *Daily News* stop-press?"

"I have not."

"I'll send one over," Gideon said. "It looks like a clash between the dockers at their dock-gate meetings and some people who call themselves the Strike Breakers, and that could mean a hell of a lot of trouble. I'll talk to City and P.L.A. to see if they've heard anything. If I can help at all, let me know."

He took the receiver from his ear, but before he replaced it he heard Upway's almost shrill "George!"

"Did you say something?" Gideon asked.

"Yes, George—who *are* these Strike Breakers? Are they Fascists?"

"I don't know anything about them. I only know that once the local Communists see the piece in that stop-press they'll be bound to have a go. So there could be a hell of a lot of trouble if we don't do something fast."

"Yes. Would you—" Upway hesitated.

Gideon, always surprised how poor one's judgment could be of people, especially those whom one did not particularly like, was surprised now. Obviously, Upway was taken off balance; as obviously he wanted some advice, yet he had never seemed to Gideon a man who would take advice gladly.

So, in a less brisk voice, Gideon said, "Would I what, Jim?"

"If you were me, would you treat this as an emergency?"

"I'd have every available man ready in case it became an emergency," Gideon said, in the most positive of voices. "Stop off duty for the next few hours and call on everyone you can get hold of. I think I'd move men from the outer-London divisions into the East End but keep 'em out of sight. Unless you've some other big job on."

"No, I haven't," Upway said. "I—er—my A.C.'s away. I'd normally see him, of course. Would you go direct to the Commissioner?"

"Once you've put the precautions in hand, yes," Gideon said.

"Thanks, George!"

"Let me know if I can help," Gideon said again.

He rang off, paused for a few moments, and then rounded his desk and sat down slowly. He wanted to see the Commissioner, of course—Sir Reginald Scott-Marle. It had been a great effort to delegate that task to Hobbs, and he was a man who lived by delegating work to others. Why did this matter? He shrugged the question off. Hobbs and Upway between them would really take over now; he had done his part. Was that what he didn't like? The fact that he couldn't see this thing through? He waited for only a few moments before putting in a call to the NE Division, where an old friend—who had once done the job which Hobbs was now doing—was in charge. This was Lemaitre, one of the real "characters" of the Force. Almost as soon as Gideon had asked for him, Lemaitre was on the line.

"Betcher I know what you're on about," he said with supreme confidence.

"Guess," said Gideon, humoring him.

"Docks, cops, and Strike Breakers!"

Gideon had to laugh.

"You'll do," he said. "You have to be right sometimes! Lem, had you heard of the Strike Breakers before this?"

"Nope," Lemaitre admitted. "But I'm going to find out P.D.Q."

"Let me know anything you come upon, will you?"

"Yes! Oh, and George, before you ring off—"

"What is it?" Gideon was anxious to get other men on the move, but showed no sign of haste or impatience. He wondered how many other Yard men or policemen in London had already heard about the impending danger.

"I had a tip from an old friend of mine at Shoreham in Sussex. He thinks a shipload of Pakistanis came ashore not far from Shoreham last night, but he's not sure and he doesn't want to raise an official alarm in case he was wrong. Bloody funny way he came onto it, as a matter of fact." Gideon was now tense with eagerness to hear the rest, but did not prompt Lemaitre. "Actually smelled them out! He was down by the old harbor—it's not used much now, only by a few fishing smacks and private yachtsmen —too much dirt and smell from the coal and oil nearby Well, he went down for a walk around one o'clock, couldn't sleep, and strolled on the breakwater There was a motor vessel of about sixty tons, fast alongside, no one aboard, hatches open. And he said the smell coming out of that hatch was curry You know, the Pakistanis eat a lot. He didn't think of it until he woke this morning— didn't identify the odor, that is. Then it dawned upon him and he called me."

"How long ago did he call?" Gideon was already near anger because much time had been wasted.

"Twenty minutes. I was just going to call you."

"Thanks." Gideon was quickly reconciled. "I'll be in touch."

He put down the receiver and picked it up again almost immediately, and when the operator answered he said, "Get me Mr. Debenham of Brighton." He put down the receiver and the internal telephone rang before he drew two breaths. He plucked it up. "Gideon."

"Commander, this is Information. We've had seven telephone calls from the divisions asking if there are any special instructions about the stop-press in the *Daily News* concerning the docks."

"Not yet, but there will be soon," Gideon said.

"Thank you, sir." Information rang off, and almost at once the same telephone rang, and when he picked it up again, a man spoke in a North Country voice. "Dale of the Back Room here, sir." The Back Room was the office of the Embankment where the Press Officer ruled and where journalists waited when they scented news. "Is there any statement about the docks situation and the so-called Strike Breakers?"

"No, but there will be soon," Gideon repeated mechanically. "How many want to know?"

"There are at least a dozen here now, sir."

"Stall them," Gideon said, "and remember that Uniform may know more than we do."

"Right, sir," said Dale.

Gideon put down the receiver and wondered how long it would be before Debenham of the Sussex Police came through. There was this sudden, fierce development in the strike emergency as well as with the immigrants, and if he knew the Yard, something else would break soon; the saying that "it never rained but it poured" was never more true than of crime. The expected bell didn't ring but the interoffice one did again, and he picked it up. There was a sense of tension peculiar to the Yard at times of crisis.

"Gideon."

"Honiwell, sir." No one could have sounded more formal or more tense—neither thing truly characteristic of the man. "Can you spare me five minutes?"

"If it's about Shoreham—"

"It's about the same subject, but in Lowestoft."

"Oh," Gideon said, startled. "Yes, come along—but our discussion may be very disjointed; it's one of those mornings." He put down the receiver and stared at the blue sky beyond the window, could not resist temptation, and got up and went to the window. The surface of the river was choppy but the sky was very bright. Traffic on the river was heavy; tugs and barges, small boats and pleasure craft were all on the move, and a police launch was chugging along

There was a tap at the passage door; this would be Honiwell.

"Come in."

Simultaneously there was a movement at the communicating door; this would be Hobbs, back already from the Commissioner.

And indeed Honiwell came in from one door and Hobbs from the other, both looking at Gideon, neither aware of the other's presence until they spoke, in unrehearsed unison.

"Sorry to worry you—" That was Honiwell.

"I thought you would like to know—" Hobbs began.

Each broke off, staring at the other in surprise; and a cross-current of wind, very strong whenever the window was open, took a door out of each hand, and so two heavy wooden doors banged simultaneously.

"Alec, you'd like to hear Superintendent Honiwell, I know. Matt, will this take long?"

"No, sir, it needn't take two minutes. I would like to go up to Great Yarmouth and Lowestoft by the first train and have Mr. Piluski with me." Piluski was the man working on the immigration investigation with him. "There's a report that a Belgian coastal vessel was hove to off the coast between Lowestoft and Great Yarmouth last night, and the bodies of two Pakistanis, dressed in Western-style lounge suits, were found in the sea off Lowestoft early this morning by coastguards. Both had died from suffocation."

The last statement hit Gideon like a physical blow. Both had died from suffocation. It was one of the things he feared, part of the horror of a situation which at times seemed to have got completely out of hand.

"How long had they been in the sea?" he asked gruffly.

"The estimate is several hours. And in view of what I reported last night"—Honiwell glanced at Hobbs, who nodded to show that he was *au fait* with that report—"I've a nasty feeling we might be on the trail of another sinking vessel with a hold crammed full of immigrants."

Gideon said, "What time's your train?"

"If I leave in five minutes, I can catch the eleven-forty-five to Lowestoft from Liverpool Street."

"Let me know what you find as soon as you get there," Gideon ordered.

"I will. Thanks." Honiwell nodded to both men and hurried out; this time, there being no cross-draft between the two doors, his closed quietly. Gideon pursed his lips and moved toward his desk, as if for the moment he had forgotten that Hobbs was there.

Hobbs did not move or speak.

Gideon sat at his desk, and said heavily, "Well, Alec, how did you get on?"

Hobbs gave the impression that he had to bring himself back to the reason for his visit, that he was seeing those bodies from the sea.

"While I was with the Commissioner, Uniform got in touch with him," he said quietly. "I heard only the one side of the conversation, but I don't think Upway will do anything rash. He's liaising with City and P.L.A., and of course I said we would do the same. We're almost certain to recognize some of the Strike Breakers, and we can use press photographs for a thorough scrutiny. The best people for photographs are the men at the *Mirror*. If we asked them to let us have some prints as soon as they're ready, they'll probably get them around to us within half an hour."

"I'll call them," Gideon promised. "All the divisions are asking for instructions. Send out a general teletype telling them we want to identify the Strike Breakers, and pick up anyone who uses an offensive weapon, will you? We'd better have as many plainclothesmen as we can muster at each gate."

"I'll see to it," Hobbs assured him.

Five minutes later, Gideon talked to the news editor of the *Mirror,* who in turn promised to rush prints around to him as soon as any were ready, asked a few pertinent questions, seemed satisfied with answers which were not answers at all, and then asked, "Where do you expect the biggest showdown, Commander?"

"Number One Gate, Saint Catharine's, is usually the storm center," Gideon answered. "But that's not to say it always will be."

"Gideon's opinion is good enough for me," the *Mirror* man declared.

The dockers put down their crates, came off the cranes, climbed out of the holds of the big and the small ships in the great Port of London, and made their way toward the dock gates, not in dozens but in hundreds. They came out of warehouses and sheds, off wharves and off bridges. They came from their homes and the pubs and the shops. They converged on the dock gates in swarms, and those who had not brought a weapon went to the hiding places and selected one. Each weapon, properly used, could cause grievous injury, while most could cause death.

The tramp of feet was like a march to war.

They laughed and joked and played the fool, the young and the old and those in middle life. They were ready for anything without knowing what anything might be.

Except for a few men who would normally be there when meetings were due, the police kept in their hiding places and, except for the plainclothesmen, did not reveal themselves.

The greatest gathering was at Number 1 Gate, St. Catharine's. There a platform had been erected and loudspeakers installed, and a protecting ring of the strongest men were about the great crowd which stood on shiny cobbles and rusty rails beneath a bright sun, hair and clothes ruffled by a strengthening breeze. Three of the strong men moved toward the platform, big Willis Mur-

doch in the middle, a giant compared with the others.
The sun glinted on his pince-nez and through his thin hair.
It was five to twelve as he stood up on the platform, and
when those at the back saw him there was a roar of ap-
plause which grew louder and louder. It became a roar as
loud as thunder; frightening and deafening.

Alan Holmes, still encased in the sleeping bag, woke
from a dazed sleep to hear the noise.

He wondered what it was, with a despairing fear

Something dreadful was happening among the dockers,
and that awareness broke through his fear for himself He
did not know how long he had been there, but the last two
or three times he had opened his eyes he had seen cracks
of daylight in the rotting roof and the wooden walls.

He was past hunger but not past thirst; his mouth was
so dry that it felt raw.

His head ached terribly and his eyes burned.

He knew that he had no chance to get out.

Above and beyond him, the din grew louder. Now
men were shouting, whistles were blowing, as if signals
were being given for an attack. They couldn't be, could
they? They couldn't be.

13

Riot

As THE DOCKERS gathered at Number 1 Gate, as the police watched, ready to step in but anxious not to precipitate any trouble, cars and small vans began to slow down at the dock approach roads, and men sprang out of them, only the driver staying and moving on to make room for the next. At the same time, men appeared from three ships already at the wharves—dozens, hundreds of men. Also at the same time, men who might have been dockers or workers from nearby factories flung grappling irons over the stone walls of the dock, so that rope ladders dangled and man after man climbed up and leaped down on the other side. In minutes, the outwardly peaceful scene became a riot—men bellowing, swearing, kicking, striking out, savage as beasts in their hatred.

For a few moments, it looked as if the police were caught unawares, in spite of the warning. It threatened to become a bloodbath; knives and knuckle-dusters, hammers and chains were out and being used with a vengeance.

Brill watched from a painter's cradle at the top of a high building not more than a hundred yards away. Two photographers were with him, including one from the *Mirror*. Newspapermen were at windows and on the nearby roofs. The invaders surged through the gates themselves as the P.L.A. policemen on duty were dragged aside; and they rushed in so that the dockers, a thousand men or more, were attacked from all directions. At the microphone, Willis Murdoch stood and talked in a voice that was a miracle of self-control.

"My advice is for you to stay at work while negotiations with the employers are proceeding. . . . We ask for a fair day's wage for a fair day's work. . . . And we ask for security. Is this security? Why have these brutes been allowed to attack us? Why . . ."

Murdoch's voice died away. Someone pulled out the cable feeding the loudspeaker, a dozen men fought their way to his platform, and six of them gathered around him in a protecting circle as the Strike Breakers hurled themselves into the attack. In three or four minutes, the whole gate area was a shambles; it did not seem as if anything could stop the fury of this battle. The noise rose up like thunder in the distance; people half a mile away heard and paused and marveled. As it grew, shrieking and screaming and crying, another noise became audible: the engines of three helicopters.

They flew at about a hundred yards from the ground, comfortably clearing the walls and the sheds and the cranes. In line, they hovered over the fighting, and from their bellies policemen appeared, firing small canisters of tear gas. At the same moment, police at the windows of the tall buildings and on the roofs of warehouses and sheds fired the same gas, and as the canisters struck walls and cobbles, as well as men and their weapons, the gas billowed out and there was an abrupt, almost incredible moment of silence, followed by gasping and choking and retching. From fighting like wild beasts in that confined area, the men ran to get out of the range of the stinging gas, and wherever they ran, they found police waiting. Black Marias, big private trucks, and lorries had been pressed into service, and the bewildered men were bundled into them without knowing what was happening. A constant stream of the big vehicles passed the open gates, only a few of the prisoners having the presence of mind to leap down for safety. The police made no great effort to stop them but drove toward one of the smaller docks, Millside, which was no longer used. There the captives were herded into big warehouses, thick with dust but weather-proof, and the police guarded the doors and the windows in great strength.

Just the same method was used at the other dock-gate battles, all with more or less the same result. At two gates, more men escaped and one lorry was seized and crashed into a wall, but that was the only setback for the police.

The screaming and the shouting died away.

The gas crept into the shed where Alan Holmes lay, and he was aware of it but it did not make him feel much worse, for he was almost beyond feeling.

What it *did* was to make the membranes of his nose swell so that breathing became more difficult. Every time he breathed in or out, he made a whistling sound.

Holmes's wife, Harriet, stood opposite Number 1 Gate as the fighting began and, when it was so suddenly quelled, began to look among the crowd for her husband but saw no sign of him. She was really worried by now, for there had been no word from him, and he had never before stayed away all night without telling her in advance. She recognized some dockers and several policemen, and watched as man after man was bundled into a waiting truck. Everyone was so busy it seemed impossible to interrupt or to speak to anyone. Not until the crowd had nearly gone did she almost give up hope, but she still fought on. Breaking from a crowd of lookers-on, she crossed to the dock gates where a group of men stood, mostly photographers, although some were policemen. There was enough gas about to sting her eyes and nostrils but not to worry her.

She recognized a Port of London Authority policeman, a man named Jackson.

"Mr. Jackson," she said, in as strong a voice as she could muster, "have you seen my husband?"

The man, big, middle-aged, very smooth-faced, looked down on her.

"Who do you mean?" he asked.

"I'm Harriet Holmes. My husband is known as—"

"Old Homer!" exclaimed one of the photographers, and she spun around to him in relief.

"Yes! Do you know where he is?"

"I haven't seen him today," the newspaperman answered, "but I often see him on his rounds."

"You mean the North Thames reporter?" asked Jackson.

"Yes." Now she swung back toward the policeman again.

That was how Malcolm Brill first saw her.

He had come down from his "cage" and had been inside the dock gates, talking to some senior police officers, who were all quietly pleased with themselves. The final number of arrests was not known, but it certainly wasn't less than seven or eight hundred. Brill, with no evening paper to telephone, would have time to write his piece in great detail for the morning *Daily News*. Already a dozen Fleet Street men had congratulated him on the stop-press item, but he had not talked much to anyone.

Everywhere he went, he saw Rose.

And everywhere he went, he saw Ledden.

He talked and listened and observed as effectively as ever, he made mental notes and put some down on paper, but he felt as if he were in two worlds: this one, where he had scored what others thought was a great triumph and which really belonged to the police, and the nightmare world, the tormenting world of last night.

He looked at the men by the gate, all shadowy figures; he saw Willis Murdoch coming from the opposite direction on a motorcycle. The next moment, he saw the woman. She wasn't at all like Rose. She wasn't beautiful. She had nice hair, very blond, and a round face and a big but shapely figure; and none of these things mattered, because he sensed that for some reason she was as distressed as he.

The photographer who had spoken to Harriet recognized him and saw Willis Murdoch at the same instant, monstrous on his little motorcycle. He put his camera to his eyes and called out, "Have you seen Old Homer, Malcolm?"

He was young and brash and anxious to impress everyone nearby with his acquaintance with a top newspaperman, and he wanted his photograph of the union leader, too. Several things happened at once. Murdoch braked his machine and nearly skidded, and the P.L.A. man Jackson said, "No need for *your* pass, Mr. Murdoch!" A little wizened red-haired man appeared from just outside the gates, and, because all those who could forbid him entry were preoccupied, slunk forward.

The woman now looked at Murdoch with pleading in her eyes.

"I saw him last night," Malcolm Brill volunteered.

"He hasn't been home," declared Harriet Holmes, in a desperate voice. "Have you seen him, Mr. Murdoch? Was he at the meeting this morning?"

It would have been easy for Murdoch to have brushed off the question; how could he reasonably be expected to see an individual in such a melee? But he got off his machine and pushed it out of the main entrance, raised its stand, and then said, "Only last night, Mrs. Holmes. D'you say he wasn't home all night?"

"No, he wasn't, and I'm terribly worried."

Yes, thought Brill, she was; out of concern and out of love for her husband, while his Rose—

He actually closed his eyes; and with them closed was aware of another, coarse voice of a man saying, *"Mr. Murdoch, can I have a word with you?"*

"In a minute, Tig," Murdoch said. "I'm sorry about this, Mrs. Holmes, I really am. When did you last see him, do you say?"

"He left about six o'clock; he said he would be seeing

you, he hoped you'd give him a story. He was worried about the strike, he couldn't really think of anything else. He—but where can he *be?*"

"Did you see him?" Murdoch turned to Brill.

"Willis, I want a word with you, it's urgent."

"Stop worrying me." Murdoch sounded unharassed by Tig's interruptions, and concerned for the woman.

Malcolm said, "Only at The Docker, when you were there."

"I saw him afterward, but I didn't talk to him—I'd been too affable to reporters already!"

"Could there have been an accident?" asked the brash reporter.

"I phoned the local hospitals and the police station and his office," Harriet informed them. "Then I thought he might have discovered something about what was going to happen this morning, and came here. I thought he was bound to be here," she added helplessly.

"Willis, you'll regret it if you don't let me have a word with you!" The voice of the wizened little man, thick with frustration, rose to a frenzy.

Brill saw Murdoch look at the man, and was surprised. He wasn't impatient or annoyed at being harassed; he was thoughtful and patient. All yesterday evening he had been, too—this militant strike leader with the pallid prizefighter's face. The eyes behind the thick-lensed pince-nez were rather pale blue.

"You'd better make it worth my while," he said mildly, and moved away from the others, while the wizened old man tottered after him.

Brill felt a curious sense of tension.

He was no longer consciously aware of his own emotional crisis; he sensed a human story, the best kind there was. He wanted to hear the other two talking but knew better than to move toward them; he also wanted to soothe Mrs. Holmes. A group of policemen with some dockers were coming toward the gate now and the rest of the men there turned to them, leaving Malcolm Brill and Harriet Holmes standing alone.

"Can you—can you do *any*thing?" the woman asked.

"If it's possible, I will," Brill promised. "And I've a feeling that Willis Murdoch will try."

"If it doesn't interfere with union business, he will," Harriet said with a touch of bitterness. "He—" She broke off, and closed her eyes; Brill recognized all the signs of a sleepless night and great emotional distress, and hoped that by simply being by her side he was some help.

Suddenly, Murdoch called, "Can you come here?" He was looking toward them while the wizened man was nodding his head to no one in particular, as if he could not be more pleased with himself.

Harriet started off, caught her foot against a broken cobble, and would have fallen but for Brill's quick grab at her waist. She steadied, wriggled her foot, and then went on, obviously not hurt. Now Willis Murdoch towered over them both. He looked more formidable, more impressive even than when he stood up in front of a crowd. No one else was within hearing.

"Mrs. Holmes," he said. "Tig here saw your husband go back to The Docker, and afterward saw him go round to the lavatory at the side. He thinks two men followed him."

"They did," asserted Tig. "I swear it, they did!"

"But where did he go?" asked Harriet tensely.

"Into the docks, *I* think," Tig said. "In fact, I could swear to it. I didn't think anything of it until I heard you asking about him, and then I said to myself—"

"Shut up, Tig," Murdoch ordered. "Mrs. Holmes, I don't want to scare you, but he is missing and there was a lot of funny business going on at The Docker last night. We all know Old Homer; if he thought there was a story, he'd go for it. Maybe he heard rumors the same as Mr. Brill did, and someone decided to stop him telling the story."

"Oh, dear God!" breathed Harriet.

"The important thing is, duck, they'd want him out of the way until after the meeting, so he might turn up any time. Easy as kiss-your-hand to shut a man up for a few hours. So what I think you ought to do is go back home in case he returns. Don't want *him* scared, in turn, do we? And Mr. Brill and me will get busy looking for him, so we can't lose."

Harriet said, in a husky voice, "You will—you will do everything, won't you?"

"I'm going to see Mr. Boyd, the employers' representative here," Murdoch said. "And Mr. Brill's going to talk to the police. They owe him a favor, and in any case they'd go to town on this job. You don't live far away, but I'll fix a car for you if you like."

"No," Harriet said decidedly. "I'll walk. I'd rather walk. I feel suffocated." She put out her hands toward the men while Tig looked on, a cretinous-looking old man. "Thank you—thank you all." She turned and hurried off, watched now by the men at the gate, for the group of police and dockers had gone.

Murdoch said, "It's only a couple of hundred yards to Boyd's office. Let's go. Tig—keep your mouth shut, understand?" He led the way as Tig gave croaking assurances, and they were soon out of earshot of everyone, although little groups of police stood about. "I didn't tell her, but Tig saw him knocked over the head last night when he came away from the privy. Instead of telling me, Tig went and drank himself into a stupor. He's only just come round and remembered."

Malcolm Brill said, "My God!"

"We need this place searched, every nook and cranny," went on Murdoch. "If you can persuade the cops to let all their men join in, I daresay I can persuade Boyd to let all the men stop working the ships to look for Old Homer. He will if he's got any sense!" Murdoch added with grim humor.

They reached the small three-story building across the

front of which ran the words "Dock Employers' Federation Offices," and within two minutes Brill was at a telephone in a small cubbyhole where he could not be overheard, and within three minutes gray-haired, long-jawed, thin-lipped Raymond Boyd of the D.E.F. was listening to Murdoch. His was a corner office on the third floor, overlooking a great expanse of the docks, the berths, the shipping, sheds, and railway tracks. Some ships were being worked and the noise of clanking and squeaking came into the office.

Boyd's desk was shaped like a horseshoe, and he sat in the middle on a swivel chair.

Murdoch, sitting in front of the desk, spoke in his usual laconic, emphatic way. These two men—foredoomed, it seemed, always to be in conflict—had both respect for and understanding of each other. No one came near them in their knowledge of the docks and the problems of labor and working methods.

When Murdoch had finished, Boyd asked, "Do you have any idea where Holmes is?"

"Not the foggiest. He could have been dumped over the side at any one of the quays, for all I know. But he might still be alive. If you—"

"I know, Willis," Boyd said, with an unexpected smile. "If I authorize all work to stop, and all personnel to join in the search—with pay," he added dryly, "with pay! Then after today's fracas everyone might be in a more flexible mood and we might get a postponement of strike action."

"Well, doesn't it stand to reason?" asked Murdoch.

"I don't know whether it's reasonable, but I'll do it," Boyd promised. "The search will have to be properly organized. Will you work with the P.L.A. force and the chaps from outside?"

"Just give me the chance," Murdoch said.

When Brill was on the telephone to the Yard, he took a chance and asked for Gideon himself, and was put through at once. He explained the situation briskly and lucidly, prepared for some exploratory questions which would give the Commander time to think.

Instead, Gideon said on the instant, "I'll send instructions to all C.I.D. men in the area to work with the dock authorities. The Uniformed people have their hands full, but they'll spare some men, I'm sure. Where can I get you if I need you?"

"I'll be at the Dock Employers' office or the Dock Workers' Union office," Brill assured him. "If I'm out with the search, someone will get a message to me. Thank you, Commander."

14

Search

POLICEMEN, NEWSPAPERMEN, white-collar workers, tally-men, railwaymen, detectives, dockers, and ships' crews who heard of the search—all joined in. One thing which quickly became apparent was the highly efficient organization on both the employers' and the employees' side. With Murdoch as virtual director of operations and the P.L.A. Chief Inspector in charge in the main dock, the whole area was divided into sections and each section put in charge of a man who knew it well enough to organize a systematic search. Even before it began, a different mood among the men became apparent. Black and white, English and Irish, Indian and Pakistani, Chinese and Greek, Italian and Spanish, but mostly native-born Londoner, went into action side by side, with the police showing a vigor and a good will which caused many people's hearts to gladden.

It warmed Willis Murdoch's.

It cheered Raymond Boyd.

It was balm to Malcolm Brill.

Every old hulk, every old shed, every crate in every warehouse, every ship's hold—all were to be searched. Every stack of fruit and provisions, every bulkhead was visited by the men who marked off the places they had searched from blueprints of the docks. Every small boat, every stack of old tires, every boilerhouse, machine shed, inspection pit, dinghy, and lifeboat was searched, and many remarkable finds were made.

In one shed was a sack of silver, tarnished over the years, obviously dumped after a robbery and never recovered. In another, a haul of small machine tools, apparently ready to be smuggled overseas. Old cars and old cycles, wallets and handbags, old shoes and socks. Old trunks and suitcases, metal boxes and attaché cases, umbrellas and walking sticks, and *seven* old perambulators —every imaginable kind of thing was found. Among piles of oranges were boxes of apples, marked for some illicit deal.

But no body was discovered, no sign of Old Homer.

Nearly every searching party passed within a few yards of him, sometimes several men at a time, but he did not know. He was oblivious of everything, unconscious. The whistling sound had stopped and there was nothing to suggest he was still breathing.

Tomcats, dead dogs, the bones of animals of many kinds and shapes and sizes added to the junk—while Harriet Holmes moved about her small house getting an early tea ready for the children, who were not yet home from school and did not know their father was missing.

As all this went on, the police began the mammoth task of charging the prisoners they had taken from the dock gates with causing or attempting to cause a breach of the peace. The total arrests, after all, were eight hundred and seventy-one, including over two hundred dockers. This was far too many to take into the police station and charge individually; too many to take into the East London Police Court the next morning, even if they could be charged. The counterblow had been a major triumph but now it was providing a major headache. Strictly speaking, it was a problem for the Public Prosecutor's office, but in fact it was a problem for the whole of the Force, not least for Gideon.

Gideon was in an unusual mood, not of dissatisfaction, disappointment, or even frustration but a combination of all three, and this unsettled him. Part of the time, he blamed his mood on the fact that his wife was away, and Penny, too. The disruption of home life was all very well for a few days, but this had been going on for nearly a week. There was much more to his mood, however. The concern and anxiety over the immigrants' situation was constant, and if he were compelled to point to one factor which affected him more than any other, it was the fear that a cargo of human beings had gone to the bottom of the North Sea.

If it had, could it have been deliberate?

The answer to that question was probably the explanation of his mood. For out of his deep knowledge of people—the warmth and goodness and generosity, as well as the coldness and the callousness—he knew that there were men evil enough to kill with such awful ruthlessness; who saw Pakistanis, Indians, Jamaicans, anyone whose skin was not white, as subhuman creatures.

The world had come a long way but in some ways it had not moved at all. The attitude of those who today dealt in immigrants and in drugs was almost identical with the slave-traders' of a century ago.

It was strange that he, Gideon, who had spent his life among criminals, and had seen human nature at its lowest, should now be so appalled by something which, had he made the effort to think, he must have known existed. Undoubtedly the way Honiwell had unburdened himself, his "I just can't keep it to myself any longer. It's beginning to prey on my mind" had stirred Gideon deeply; and the story itself had shocked as well as horrified him. Now he began to wonder if he could have prevented any disaster by giving the matter deeper, more concentrated thought.

He could not remember a time when any particular case was all-pervasive, influencing his thinking about all others and lessening the impact of some. He did not feel the great lift which affected nearly everyone at the Yard as the news of the triumph at the docks came in. He should have been there, of course; it would have done him a world of good.

In the middle of the afternoon, as reports of the identity of the men arrested at the docks were trickling through, a number of factors preoccupied him, and to get his mind clear, as well as to try to overcome the mood, he put them down on paper in a series of headings:

1. Bank robbery at Clerkenwell—arrest expected.
2. Missing newspaperman at Number 1 Gate—no news.
3. Sussex coast suspect shipload of immigrants—no news.
4. Honiwell—no news, but he would not be at Lowestoft yet.
5. Cache of heroin and cannabis found in Hampstead hotel.

There wasn't much there; not really much.

Gideon stared at the list for at least five minutes, a new thought stirring in his mind. There wasn't much there— he had delegated virtually everything. He wasn't personally enough involved. He had given most of the briefing—as over the bank robbery—to Hobbs. He himself and his life at the Yard were going through a period of transition. *That* was surely at the root of his strange mood. That and the fact that since Malcolm Brill of the *Daily News* had called, his telephones had been silent. The great tides which swept through Scotland Yard were leaving him high and dry.

"I haven't enough to do," he said aloud. "I've too much time to think!"

When one of three telephones on his desk rang—that which came through from the Yard's exchange—it actually made him jump. He picked the receiver up quickly, even eagerly, and heard the Inspector who cleared calls for him and Hobbs say, "Here is Mr. Gideon."

"Who wants me?" asked Gideon.

"Commander," Mesurier of the *Daily News* said. "Lord Nagel of the Unity Press group is not uninterested in the problem you were discussing last night. I thought it safe to tell him that you had organized the dock coup, and I've no doubt that impressed him. While Unity Press isn't the biggest of the popular groups, it is very big, and the *Daily Star*, its chief daily, is very much a 'cause' newspaper."

Gideon felt his heart lifting.

"I think he would have been interested even without the outstanding success at the docks today," Mesurier went on "Are you by chance free to dine with him and me tonight to discuss the whole immigrant situation and what you think Unity Press could do to help?"

Gideon already felt as if he had been given a new lease on life

"Yes," he said "I'll be free anytime, anywhere."

Mesurier gave an unexpected, pleasing chuckle. "You really are the greatest enthusiast I know!" he said. "Lord Nagel's home, 21 Hanover Terrace, Hyde Park—at seven o'clock, then."

"Wonderful!" said Gideon.

He put down the receiver but before he was aware of the full impact of the news, before he could even begin to relish it properly, the phone rang again, quivering beneath his hand He let it ring for a moment, thinking how much he would like to talk to Honiwell about this. Slowly he put the receiver to his ear and as slowly announced his name.

A man with a mellifluous voice uttered one word and contrived to make it sound like a whole sentence. The word was "Congratulations "

Deliberately obtuse but instantly aware of the beautifully turned-out man whom he had met in Fleet Street yesterday afternoon, Gideon asked, "On what? And who is that?"

"Nigel Simply," the other announced, in the same tone; he sounded half amused but at the same time very earnest. "And my congratulations are on the success of your dock maneuvers."

"I'm sure everyone at Scotland Yard will be grateful," Gideon said dryly.

"I mean you personally, Commander. You did inspire the stop-press paragraph in the *Daily News,* this morning, didn't you?"

"I asked the newspaper to send a good man along to find out what he could," Gideon answered. "If that is inspiring anything, all right."

Simply chuckled, quite deep in his throat.

"The hero who won't admit being one! Commander, I am going to write my version of your part in this affair in my column for tomorrow, and I wondered if you would care to give me a little other information about a variety of things. If I came to see you, could you spare me a few minutes?"

Gideon almost said, "No," and dithered for several seconds while the man at the other end of the line waited. Finally Gideon pushed his lips into the mouthpiece, and answered, "If you don't mind the risk of wasting your time, yes."

"I will most certainly take that minimal risk! May I come at once?"

"Yes," Gideon said. "I'll leave word in the hall that you're to be brought straight along." He rang off on Simply's "Thank you" and in the same movement picked up the internal telephone. Now things were moving at the kind of speed he was used to, and he was in a buoyant mood. Even when Sir Reginald Scott-Marle, the Commissioner, answered in his familiar aloof-sounding voice, buoyancy was the keynote in Gideon's. "Gideon here, sir," he said.

"George," said Scott-Marle, "the docks result was most rewarding and the method masterly."

"Sir Giles Rook and Lawless of the Port of London Authority—" began Gideon.

"I know exactly what happened. The City Commissioner telephoned me half an hour ago." Having silenced Gideon, Scott-Marle went on dryly, "But I'm sure that isn't what you wanted to talk about."

"Not exactly," Gideon conceded, just as dryly. "But some things are related. Am I needed in the roundup of the prisoners, do you know?"

"No. Hobbs and Upway are coping, and of course the divisions and the police courts are the main centers. The problem is how to hold so many prisoners overnight, and the answer seems to be to set up some special courts. Hobbs will be in touch with you."

"Thank you, sir," Gideon said. "The next thing is very different. Nigel Simply of the *Examiner* has probably guessed that I put the *Daily News* onto the dock business, and is going to write it up."

"Good!" ejaculated Scott-Marle.

"You don't mind?"

"Every paragraph we can get about this to our credit is good," Scott-Marle declared. "If some of them draw attention to you, I shall be very glad. Your light is too often hidden under a bushel." For the reserved Scott-Marle, this comment was almost skittish, and it told Gideon the measure of the importance of what had been achieved.

"After Simply it may shine too brightly," Gideon remarked. "He is coming here to see me in the next twenty minutes or so. Is there any particular way in which you would like me to steer him?"

Scott-Marle gave a chuckle of sheer enjoyment.

"George," he said, "if you can steer Nigel Simply, it will be a greater triumph even than the docks! Don't worry about what you tell him or what he gets out of you —and least of all, what he publishes." After leaving time for that to soak in, Scott-Marle asked, in a voice and manner more characteristic of him, "Do any other issues worry you?"

"My biggest worry is the illegal immigration," Gideon replied.

"That I can well understand. Is there anything more we can do, as far as you know? Can do without risking any kind of conflict with the Home Office, I mean." The Home Office was an ever-present bogey in the face of Scotland Yard, and sooner or later all men chafed under the restrictions it imposed, even the Commissioner.

"Not officially," Gideon answered. "But I am going to try to persuade the *Daily Star* to take it up as a cause and use all the pressure it can, as well as arouse public opinion. It will be a confidential attempt, of course, but if it should leak out that I am trying to persuade a newspaper to put pressure on our masters——" He broke off, suddenly aware of the full gravity of what he was doing, and as suddenly aware that on this issue Scott-Marle might think he had gone too far. The silence which followed made this seem even more likely. He sat rigid, rocklike, not knowing what he would do if Scott-Marle virtually ordered, "Don't do it."

"George," the Commissioner said, at last; the "George" meant at least that he had not taken umbrage. "Let me have a written note about this, and put in the remark you made when we last talked about this: that you feel this is not wholly a police matter and that in order to resolve it, a nationwide survey of immigrant housing, living, and working conditions should be made by the Ministry and by local authorities. If anything should leak out about what you're doing, then I shall be able to show that you had informed me. If challenged, I can point out that I had had no time to make any recommendation. So we are both covered from sniping attacks in the House."

Gideon thought with a rush of emotion, He's for this as much as I am!

"I'll do that note right away," he promised gruffly.

"Thank you," said Scott-Marle. "Let me know what happens in the morning."

"I will, sir. Goodbye." Gideon rang off, and sat back for a moment while a tension he had not been aware of eased from his body. Then he stood up and moved to the window, looking out on the river, which was much calmer now, although the sky was overcast and everything looked cold. In the space of half an hour, he had received more encouragement than he had dreamed possible. Now what he had to do was use it to the best possible advantage. What the devil had been the matter with him—not enough to do! He gave a snort of a laugh and turned away from the window, rang the secretarial pool, and asked for a Miss Sabrina Sale.

"I think she's free, Commander. Shall I send someone else if she isn't?"

"Provided whoever comes knows that it's an urgent job and might mean working late."

"I'll see to it, sir." The manageress of the pool rang off, while Gideon went through a filing cabinet and ruffled through folders until he came to one marked "Immigration Draft Report." He took this out and read it quickly; it carried all the recommendations Scott-Marle had recalled, and there was nothing in it he would change. He picked up a ballpoint pen and wrote in one corner, "Copies for the Commissioner, Mr. Hobbs, Mr. Honiwell, Mr. Piluski, 2 spares," and finished as there was a tap at the door. On his "Come in," a pleasant-looking, attractive woman came in, with soft, graying hair and soft, pleasing skin. She wore pince-nez but they seemed right for her. She wore a plain pink blouse and a knee-length pleated black skirt.

"Commander."

"Come in, Sabrina." Gideon pointed to a chair. "I want you to go over that draft report on immigration, and put any obvious mistakes right—you know what my syntax is like!—and get me some copies very quickly."

"Of course," she promised.

"And there's just one letter," Gideon went on, and the woman crossed nice legs and rested her notebook on her knee. "To the Commissioner, copy Mr. Hobbs. Further to the report which I enclose, I should advise you that I have an opportunity of discussing some aspects of this prob-

lem with Lord Nagel, Chairman of Unity Press Enterprises, and Mr. Charles Mesurier of the *Daily News*. I
will report the results of these discussions as soon as
practicable."

He finished.

He was aware that Sabrina Sale was looking up at him,
smiling very gently. She was an attractive woman, and in
different circumstances they might have become close
friends. As it was, they knew each other well within the
limitations of the Yard. Her gray eyes also smiled, and
she seemed about to stretch out her right hand.

Then she drew back, and asked quite briskly, "Is that
everything, Commander?"

"Yes. Can you get it done by half past five?"

"I don't know," she said. "But I'll stay as late as
necessary to get it finished. Do you—do you really think
it possible that you *will* get some action? If you could, it
would be by far the greatest thing even you have ever
done."

He had no doubt at all that she meant every word,
and was more affected than he could say. He almost resented the sharp ring of the telephone bell; but it came,
and he moved to take it as Sabrina Sale turned away.

15

Shipload *Desdemona*

GIDEON PUT THE RECEIVER to his ear, said "Gideon," and watched the door close on the woman's surprisingly attractive figure.

The next moment, a man with a familiar voice said in a tone of controlled excitement, "Ten to one you don't know what I've got, George!"

It was Lemaitre in a gleeful mood, and he could often be gleeful and triumphant without any good reason. Gideon had to make an effort to humor him.

"What have you found?"

"A cellarful of immigrants!" Lemaitre almost brayed.

The significance, even the actual words, did not strike Gideon at first. The way the phrase was uttered made it sound like the words of a song: "A Pocketful of Miracles." "A Cellarful of Immigrants." Then the meaning dawned on him as if it had been hammered into his mind.

Before he could speak, before he really began to feel anger at the flippant way Lemaitre made the announcement, Lemaitre went on in an urgent tone, "George, I didn't mean to sound like a cackling old hen. And I *mean* it. It's that load from Brighton, I'll betcha—from the *Desdemona* or some such name. We got a teletype asking us to look for a pale gray Volkswagen minibus with the blinds drawn—Brighton or was it Folkestone sent it out?"

"Brighton," Gideon answered, his anger fading. There

was some indication that a minibus had left the jetty where the curry-smelling ship was tied up. "And you found it?"

"Yes. One of our chaps noticed a minibus backed up against a door in a house in Quill Street—you know, just behind the Whitechapel Road. Something was being loaded or unloaded in a hurry. He didn't tackle the van then but sent word back, and the van was picked up, empty, twenty minutes ago. It reeks with curry and pomade. We've held the driver, who says he delivered a lot of Pakistanis or Indians to the house, and thought they were going down into the cellar."

"Thought!" Gideon barked.

"Oh, they're there all right," Lemaitre said with scornful confidence. "That bus was crowded—he reckons there were over fifty in it, twice as many as there should be. The question is, do we pick them up now or wait in case the men who fixed all this turn up? Someone's bound to, even if it's only a go-between; they won't leave them to rot."

Gideon caught himself about to say, "Don't be too sure," and replied with brisk positiveness: "Have the place surrounded. Make arrangements in advance for all the immigrants to be taken to a school or a hall where they can be given some food and not frightened out of their lives. Keep me posted stage by stage, I—oh! Don't collect them in Black Marias, use a couple of buses."

Lemaitre said, as if puzzled, "Taking a lot of trouble, George, aren't you?"

"Yes. Fix it, Lem," Gideon ordered.

"Oh, I'll fix it, don't you worry!" Lemaitre rang off as if to impress Gideon with his zeal, while Gideon felt a curious sensation, half satisfaction, half nausea. How could human beings be treated like cattle in this day and age? Then, with a switch of mood: Well, this lot's all right, thank God.

He thought of Honiwell, and the shipload of Pakistanis Honiwell believed to be in acute danger. It did not occur to him any more than it had occurred to Lemaitre that there might be danger for the men who had been smuggled into the country from the S.S. *Desdemona* on the south coast.

Then the door opened and a messenger said, "You did say Mr. Simply was to be brought straight up, sir, didn't you?"

Good Lord, thought Gideon. He had forgotten Nigel Simply!

The most bitter and angry, spiteful, vengeful, and dangerous man in England, at that time, was a middle-aged Englishman named John Winfrith. He was one of the few English people who could trace his ancestry back to the era before the Norman Conquest; but a series of misalliances in his family and the divers wars had so adulterated the Saxon blood that his father had been bitter before him, and had taught his son bitterness.

"We should be able to take our seats with the highest in the land, but when the third baron married that Russian bitch, he began the decline, for the baronetcy died. Don't be under any illusion, John. The blood of your children should be kept pure. Mixed marriages are made in hell and the children of them live in hell."

Every single thing that went wrong in the affairs of the country, the father had blamed on mixed marriages: the marriages of sin. In the son's youth there had been very few unions between black and white; his early prejudices had been against mixed marriages with Jews and with Europeans whatever their nationalities. But after the Second World War, when the father had died in a bombing raid, John Winfrith had seen the new flood of immigrants from Jamaica, Hong Kong, and Singapore, and eventually from India and Pakistan.

He did not, at first hate the people themselves.

But as the months and the years passed, he grew to hate them.

And as the months and the years passed, a new hatred

grew within him: for those who accepted the situation without protest.

Moreover, as the economy of the nation grew weaker and its problems greater, he began to hate not only those who came from other lands, but all whom he blamed for the watering down of the greatness of Britain. The Socialists. The trades unions. The workers. There had never been much reason in him, and there was less and less as the years wore on. He had, however, two great assets.

He was wealthy: his father had been most astute in stock exchange dealings and in land speculation and had left him six million pounds, after estate duty had been paid. And he was not only wealthy but a clever and shrewd organizer, and a good judge of men.

Without becoming associated with any extreme political group, he had gathered about him a number of extreme right-wingers and had for years organized a constant supply of mercenaries to and from the lands in Africa, the Middle East, and South America, where they would be hired to fight on the side of right-wing forces, whether in the government or as revolutionaries. He was well informed, having built up a system of well-paid spies, and knew whenever a particular war was going one way or the other; if badly, he drew his men out. They were trained, tough, and believers in might, which they had seen triumph over and over again.

Slowly, he trained them to work in England, for he had always had a dream of serving England, and believed he could do this best in two ways. First: rid the nation of strikes. Second: rid the nation of colored immigrants in particular and all immigrants in general.

He believed that once these two objectives were attained, he would have changed the life of the nation. He had no great dreams of political power. He was not a Fascist in the sense that he believed in permanent domination by a group of right-wing extremists. He just saw these two factors as cancers in the body of England, and believed that once they were out the body would recover and democracy would become healthy. To achieve this end he believed in might, and believed in the power of fear.

It had not occurred to him even in his most pessimistic moments that the attacks at the docks would lead to such a disaster. He had thought that with a series of commando or mercenary raids on the dockers he would frighten them into coming to terms with the employers. He had selected the docks because they were the main artery of trade, and he had plans for similar attacks on car factories and other big plants where strikes were commonplace. He had pictured a sensational success at the docks, and when the Strike Breakers' actions were under way, he planned to move his main attack onto first the illegal and then the legal immigrants. Quite cold-bloodedly, he planned the sinking of known shiploads of Indians and Pakistanis, and to make sure he was fully informed he bought his way into the European syndicates which were extorting large sums from the immigrants on promises of a passage to England and trouble-free entry into the land.

So he knew about the passengers crowded into the S.S. *Desdemona*.

He also knew about the others battened down into the stinking hold of the SS. *Breem* in the North Sea.

He knew that the easiest victims, for him, were those on the S.S. *Breem*, and he did not intend them to land. Already rumors of shiploads of these immigrants being sunk were spreading, and his agents spread them skillfully, so that they caused much alarm in those parts of England where the nonwhite population was thickest—in some areas, as high as 50 percent of the total population. Everything had been going according to plan.

His method with the passengers from the S.S. *Desdemona* was different.

He proposed to get them in, deliver them to a rendezvous in London—in fact, a cellar which spread under three houses in Whitechapel—and leak their presence to the police so that they would undoubtedly be sent back to Pakistan. Now, however, his agents had told him that the police had traced his shipload and the Volkswagen bus, and might get onto them—and so onto him—at any time.

He was suffering from the first overwhelming defeat in his life.

He could see his plans crashing about him.

He knew that among the arrested men were over four hundred of his own, who had been trained in all kinds of fighting but who had been overwhelmed by the surprise intervention of the police on such a scale.

He hated the police, the dockers, the Pakistanis: he was ablaze with hate.

He was a small man, with beautiful pale hair more silver than white, a pink complexion; and he was in his middle fifties, although he looked no more than forty. He had clear blue eyes, and could appear as innocent as a boy in the choir stalls. None would have suspected that he was so consumed with hate.

The agent, a man named David, who telephoned him about the passengers from the S.S. *Desdemona* was puzzled by his silence after the report—that the police had traced the van to the houses concerned and doubtless would soon stage a raid. So the agent remarked with a forced laugh, "They're as tight-packed in that cellar as they were in the ship."

"Yes," Winfrith said. "I know. Where are you?"

"I'm in a telephone booth at the end of Quill Street," the agent said. "I can see the house from here."

"David," Winfrith said, "I've some bad news."

"*More* bad news?"

"Some of those blacks in the cellar could give the police information which could lead back to us."

"My God!" exclaimed the man. "What are we going to do?"

"The ventilation holes are at the back, aren't they?"

asked Winfrith. "If someone dropped a couple of those old containers of phosgene down one, they wouldn't be able to talk to anybody. If I were nearer, I'd do it myself."

"Don't you worry," David said hoarsely. "I'll fix those black bastards."

Chief Detective Superintendent Lemaitre, in charge of NE Division of the Metropolitan Police, knew Gideon better, perhaps, than any man in the Force except Alec Hobbs. Lemaitre had been Gideon's chief assistant during Gideon's early days as the Commander C.I.D., and had learned to judge his moods and mannerisms extremely well. When he replaced the receiver after talking to Gideon that afternoon, he sat back in his chair. He was a long-legged, bony-faced man, with sparse, sleek hair and a thin neck; he wore a polka-dot red-and-white tie and a pepper-and-salt-colored lounge suit.

"George is after someone's blood," he remarked to the empty room. "I don't want it to be mine!" He gave all the necessary orders, and then checked that they were being put in hand at once. It would take half an hour to surround the houses, he judged, but longer to lay on the buses or coaches. There was just a chance that a small firm of car- and coach-hire people, not a stone's throw away, would have two spare coaches for an hour.

He called the owner, and explained his problem.

"Got just the thing for you, skipper," the man said. "Two single deckers, come in for a spring clean and a paint job, general overhaul. They'll be just right. From where to where, did you say?"

"Quill Street to Mickleson Hall," Lemaitre replied. "Shouldn't take much more than an hour. Have the buses there in half an hour, will you?"

"No problem at all," the other assured him.

Lemaitre rang off and rubbed his hands, very satisfied, but aware of one weak link in his chain. Mickleson Hall was part of a youth-club complex and was equipped with foam-rubber mattresses, chairs, and emergency supplies, and was used for emergency evacuations. Twice it had been used when fire had swept crowded tenement areas, once when a high-rise building in a new apartment complex had threatened to collapse. It was used for a variety of purposes during the day and evenings.

He called the warden of the club.

"How long will you need it for?" the man asked.

"Well, I dunno—could be overnight, could be two or three days." Lemaitre was already prepared for objections, equally prepared to use Mickleson Hall for a few hours while he sought out a place for a longer term.

He heard a rustling of pages before the man said, "We've two club groups there tonight and one tomorrow but I can shift them. Otherwise it's available for the weekend. Will that be long enough?"

"That's the ticket!" exclaimed Lemaitre. "Thanks, Charlie. If we have our party there in an hour, say, will that be all right??"

"Yes," the other replied. "They'll need some food, and —but leave that to me."

Lemaitre rang off, jubilantly convinced that Gideon would be delighted; it was almost as if Gideon could see and hear him now. He got up and went downstairs, checking with his Chief Inspector that the cordon was either in position or would be very soon.

"Then let's go!" cried Lemaitre, clapping his hands with a bang.

"Are you coming, sir?" The Chief Inspector looked astonished.

"You don't think I would miss this, do you?" Lemaitre demanded.

Winfrith's man David, with the phosgene containers safe in his pocket, knew that he had only just time to get the job done and make his escape. He wore a peaked cap and a suit that was too large for him, and, with an expertise born of long practice, had stuck on sideburns and a mustache, which made him look very different from his usual self. He had no fear at all of being recognized; the only problem was to get to the ventilator grille where he'd be out of sight of the police. He was trained in guerrilla warfare and had physical courage, or indifference to danger, which probably explained why he held the life of others so cheaply.

The three small houses were in a terrace which had been condemned, and the cellar had been converted to hold a lot of people; the ventilation holes were at the back, approached over rubble of what had once been other houses. Close by was a new estate, all about it narrow roads of terraced houses, like these, from which the police watched.

David picked his way toward the shaft.

Lemaitre and his Chief Inspector pulled into the end of the street as the two coaches appeared at the other end. The police, only watching until then, began to move in.

David realized that the raid was coming more quickly than he had expected, and he broke into a run. Where most men would have given up, he became more determined than ever to "fix those black bastards." Several police started after him but no one at first worried about him—he seemed just a man loitering and, like many in this part of the world, nervous of the police.

It was Lemaitre, watching, who said sharply, "That chap's up to no good! He's heading for the houses." The Chief Inspector, only a second behind his chief in sensing the same thing, swung off the road and onto the rubble. The tires crunched and rumbled, the springs creaked. David turned his head and saw the car heading toward him when he was only twenty feet from the ventilation hole. Other policemen, on foot, now began to run. He pulled the two containers out of his pocket, and hurled one toward the ventilation hole but he missed by a foot. As the car slowed down and the door opened, he hurled the second one at the man who got out: Lemaitre. Lemaitre wasn't in a position in which he could duck or do anything to protect himself, and the fragile container struck him on the chest.

But it did not break.

Two police men converged on David, who now simply tucked his elbows into his sides and ran. Lemaitre, struggling to his feet, saw gas creeping out of the other container and hugging the ground, and saw two of his men kicking at the thing. It wasn't until after he had sent an SOS for gas masks that he realized they were kicking it away from the ventilation shaft.

The men who had been smuggled in did not get even a whiff of the gas, which was easily confined to a small area because there was no wind.

They were appalled by the fact that they were suddenly in the hands of the police, and even the comforts of Mickleson Hall and the food and ministrations from a local colony of Pakistanis did little to soothe them.

16

$$\underline{}$$

SOS

GIDEON SAT BACK behind his desk, smiling faintly. The interview between him and Nigel Simply had become, in a way, a battle of wits—Simply continually probing, Gideon fending off questions which he did not think could be answered effectively. The other man, wearing a puce-colored suède suit, a flowing psychedelic tie, and a pale pink shirt, looked an exquisite; but he would have made a brilliant barrister.

He said, after half an hour, "Now that I know the subjects you don't want to talk about, Commander, do tell me what you *would* like me to print. I promise not to quote you in self-praise but show you personally in a good light! However, I *do* need spice, and you have been masterfully evasive in comment about the structure of the Yard, its hierarchy, and its methods. There must surely be something which you feel could be changed to advantage."

Gideon said, "At least, improved."

"Very well, improved. Won't you commit yourself at least to one fantasy dream you would bring to reality if you could do so by waving a wand? And I don't mean doubling the Establishment or trebling the pay or improving working conditions. Buying the most up-to-date equipment for your laboratory and photography departments, for instance, which I am told are somewhat ante-diluvian. Or even the somewhat anachronistic habit of calling all senior officers 'sir.' Don't you think the homage to rank can be overdone these days?"

"Respect for and homage to are different things," Gideon replied, but he was looking very intently at the other man now, and, sensing a change in his mood, Simply made no comment and asked no question. "Yes. There is one thing I would do if I could wave a wand."

"Ah!" said Simply. "Why don't you wave one and see what happens? And may I quote whatever you are about to say?"

"Yes," Gideon agreed flatly. He paused, so as to phrase his words with great care. "The police in general have too many borderline cases to deal with. We are often not really sure what is within our province and what isn't. Society has changed enormously in the past twenty or thirty years, but the police haven't been changed to cope." He was aware that he was groping for words, after all, and began to wish he hadn't committed himself. He pushed his chair back and moved to the window, in that favorite aid-to-thought position. After a few moments, he went on: "Perhaps this is the best way to put it. We have a dual task, of crime detection and crime prevention. For the most part, we can and do handle the detection side of it reasonably well. We could do an infinitely better job if much more time was available to concentrate on methods of crime prevention. We, as a police force, aren't really equipped to do this. It is a matter first for the Home Office and then for the local authorities. Social conditions can and do breed crime. I don't simply mean poverty and slums, which, except in some areas where immigrants are the victims, are mostly things of the past. I mean such things as excessively permissive attitudes to drugs, to sex, to smuggling, to tax evasion. There is, I am sure, a direct relation between certain kinds of crime and the high rate of tax. The conditions for all of these social conditions are created by society—by politicians, if you like. We, the police, too often have to deal with the consequences. Over five hundred police were at or near the docks today, with twice as many in reserve, and I've no doubt at all that crime—such as shoplifting, housebreaking, the looting of telephone meters—all leaped up in the rest of London. We aren't really used simply for crime detection, or prevention, however. Either would be comparatively easy. We have to try to hold a line where our society has broken down. And once the public and, for that matter, the politicians know that, the more the police will be seen in their right perspective."

During this, Nigel Simply sat absolutely still. Gideon was aware of him but had a sense of understanding: of this man being *simpatico*. When at last he stopped, he felt satisfied that he had said what was in his mind in the best way he could. He believed it had needed saying. He moved away from the window to the desk, groping in his pocket for the big-bowled pipe which he never smoked. He took it out and smoothed it in his palm.

At last, Simply stirred.

"Commander," he said. "Thank you. I am completely committed to helping you in whatever way I can."

He stood up, and shook hands and went out, as if, there being nothing else to say, he did not want to linger. Gideon was reassured—in fact, as warmed by this man's words as he had been by Sabrina Sale's. He closed the door on him, wishing he had phrased the peroration differently and changed the places of emphasis, but these were trifles. Before long he heard the direct external telephone ring; almost at once the instrument which was connected to the Yard's exchange rang. He picked up the external one, said "A moment, please," and then picked up the other. "Gideon," he announced.

"George," Lemaitre said, "some bastard tried to kill them. Used some World War I phosgene. We stopped him, though. They're all dossed down at Mickleson. But it shook me to the guts."

"What happened to the man?" Gideon demanded.

"We've got him in the cells here. Won't give his name,

won't talk, won't do a flicking thing. Want to see him yourself?"

"Possibly," Gideon said thoughtfully. "But you and I will talk before long; I've another call waiting. Are you all right yourself?"

"Never been better," Lemaitre assured him.

Gideon said mechanically, "Good. I'll call you back." In fact, it was not until he had replaced the receiver that the full implications struck home. "Some bastard tried to kill them. Used some World War I phosgene." Good God, what *was* happening? He almost forgot the other call, actually began to replace that receiver, and heard a voice coming from it. Hastily, he put it back to his ear.

"Gideon."

"It's Honiwell," said Honiwell, in a voice that seemed charged with tension. "I heard most of that—it was Lemaitre, wasn't it?"

"Yes."

"Was he talking about some Pakistanis who came in last night?"

"Yes."

"George," said Honiwell, "four more bodies have been washed up along the coast here. There's no trace of the S.S. *Breem,* the ship which was standing off last night. What I want is an air-sea search, and the local C.C. is agreeable if the Yard is."

After a brief pause, Gideon said, "The Yard is. I'll call Colonel Starr."

"I knew you wouldn't waste any time," Honiwell said, with obvious relief. "There are still a few hours of daylight left." He paused while Gideon picked up the telephone from the Yard exchange and said, "Get me Colonel Starr of the Defence Ministry at once."

"Thanks," Honiwell said. "I—Geo—sorry. What's really happened in London, sir? All kinds of wild rumors are flying about here."

"The attack on the dockers was a flop," Gideon said. "We made over eight hundred arrests and special courts will sit this evening. Lemaitre found where the men off the *Desdemona* had been taken—but you heard that. Now my other phone's ringing, and that's probably Starr. Where are you?"

"Lowestoft Police Headquarters, with Superintendent Cressy."

"I'll call back or arrange for a message," Gideon said, and then his voice rose. "No! Hold on. If this is Starr, we can save time." He picked up the other receiver, and schooled his voice to be less peremptory, just saying, "Gideon here." It was Colonel Starr, a recently appointed liaison officer between the military and any help that was needed by the police or Home Office. Starr listened to the straightforward request, and said, "It can be arranged from Mildenhall and Great Yarmouth. You can be sure it will be started at once, Commander. What did you say your man's name is up there?"

"The man you want is Superintendent Cressy. My chap is Honiwell."

"I know Honiwell," said Starr. "Don't worry, Commander."

"I can't thank you enough."

"Nonsense!" Starr said gruffly. "On a day like today, we begin to understand more of what we owe to you chaps."

As if half regretting the compliment, the liaison officer rang off, leaving Gideon smiling faintly. He could not remember a day when praise and compliments had come so freely and from such unexpected sources. He must be careful; pride still came before a fall.

He put his lips closer to the other telephone and asked, "Did you get that, Matt—it's in hand."

"I got it," Honiwell said. "I'm glad you put him on to Cressy, who's a good chap but a bit conscious of his position. I'll be in touch," he promised. "Good night."

Gideon said, "Good night," and glanced at his watch as he put down the receiver, then realized the other receiver wasn't back on its holder. He replaced it noisily.

The time was six o'clock; there was just under an hour before he need start for Lord Nagel's place, and he toyed with the idea of going home and changing. He decided against it, took a clean shirt and a different tie and two handkerchiefs out of a drawer in his main desk, and placed them near the telephone; he would go up to the washrooms and change soon. Sabrina Sale hadn't yet brought him the report and the letter; he probably hadn't allowed her enough time. Hobbs wasn't back, and he would have liked a report. He rang for Hobbs in case he had just come into his office, but there was no response; of course Hobbs would tell him the moment he returned.

The exchange telephone rang, and Gideon answered mechanically, "Gideon."

"I'm sorry I haven't been back, Commander," Hobbs said, his tone telling Gideon that someone else was with him. "The job of sorting out the wheat from the chaff, as it were, is taking longer than we expected. Can you spare half an hour, by any chance?"

In spite of what had happened, in spite of the chorus of praise, in spite of the realization of his changing role in the affairs of the Yard, Gideon's heart leaped. To his dying day there would be nothing so good or so satisfying as participation in any kind of actual police work; and there was real pleasure in the thought that he might be useful, and therefore needed.

"Where?" he asked.

"Whitechapel," Hobbs said. "The old Regality Cinema. About two hundred men were brought here from the docks—the roughest and most difficult to handle. The dockers who have their union cards are being sent to the special East London sitting, and they'll be bound over. But most of them aren't dockers, and carry no identification. Willis Murdoch, the union leader, has taken a close look at them and swears they've never been at the docks as workers. The *Mirror* photographs are here, and where we can identify a man who jumped out of a van or climbed the walls, we're holding him overnight for the morning court. But—well, you and Lemaitre will need to decide which are the Strike Breakers and who got mixed up by accident. Lemaitre's on his way."

"I'll come," Gideon said. "I won't have much time, but I'll come." He put down the receiver with a bang and looked at the shirt and oddments on the desk; there wouldn't be a chance to change now—in fact, he would be late for dinner at Lord Nagel's. He moved toward the door as it opened, and backed from Sabrina Sale, who carried a sheaf of papers. "Just the thing I need," Gideon said, moving toward the desk and speaking before she put the papers down in front of him. "Will you telephone the *Daily News* and make sure that Mr. Mesurier knows I'll probably be late for dinner? Not very late, but a little. Tell him we're in a tangle over the special courts in the East End, and I'm helping to sort it out." He sat down and skimmed through the letter to Scott-Marle while she thumbed a telephone directory for the *News* number. By the time he had signed the note, she was asking for Mesurier; obviously she got him. The letter said exactly what he meant to say to Scott-Marle, but it gave him second thoughts about what he had said to Nigel Simply. If Simply used that—well, in for a penny, in for a pound! He turned to the door.

Sabrina Sale rang off, and asked, "Don't you want these?"

"These what—oh, the shirt. No time," said Gideon, opening the door. "Phone down for a car for me, will you?"

"No time for what?" She followed him out of the office.

"To change. Sabrina—"

"Take them with you," she said, thrusting them into his arms. "Surely you can change a shirt in the car coming back? And *please* don't be too late at that dinner," she pleaded, hurrying to keep pace by his side. "It's far more important in the long term than anything in the short term."

"I won't be too late," he said, *"if* I don't have to wait for a car."

She fell behind at one of the other offices, and he glanced over his shoulder and saw her disappearing into it. She wasn't looking his way. He hoped he hadn't upset her by his brusqueness. It was odd how one could worry about a woman subordinate and not worry at all about a man. He ducked into one of the lavatories, washed, pondered the advisability of changing, and decided there simply wasn't time. No one was in sight, but when at last he reached the bottom of the big flight of steps, a car was already nosing forward, and stopped as he drew level.

"Don't get out," he ordered, opening the door. "Just turn off left on the Embankment." He climbed into the car and sat back heavily, and then more by luck than judgment glanced up the steps. "Wait a minute!" he called, for Sabrina Sale was hurrying down them, carrying what looked like a big piece of brown paper. He opened the window as she reached the car, and before he could comment or question, Sabrina thrust the paper inside. It was a shopping bag.

"For the dirty clothes," she said breathlessly. "But *do* change, Commander, and please do try not to be too late."

She backed away, looking both pleasing and pleading.

He called after her "I won't!" and sat back, chuckling to himself as he pushed the shirt into the big shopping bag. "I wonder where she got it from," he said aloud, then leaned forward and spoke to the driver. "The old Regality Theatre, Whitechapel. Do you know it?"

"Did all my youthful courting there, sir," the driver replied.

Gideon chuckled again.

But there was nothing remotely amusing at the cinema theatre, which was now closed and had huge FOR SALE notices written and plastered all over it in hideous colors. Outside was a cordon of police, and there were police at

the back and side entrances, too. In the foyer were Hobbs;
Upway, so tall and whippetlike to look at; and several
officers from Lemaitre's division; and, at one side, perhaps a dozen newspapermen were waiting. Among these
Gideon noticed Malcolm Brill. Willis Murdoch and two
other union officials were there, obviously set on getting
the dockers' charges reduced and the hearings over
quickly.

Gideon thought, I've forgotten that man who disappeared. He shook hands with several of the policemen,
whom he hadn't seen for years, and went with Hobbs
toward a wall covered with photographs set in panels
once used for the glamour pictures of film stars. He saw
that the photographs were riot and pre-riot scenes, and
at a distance they seemed excellent. The *Mirror* had
really gone to town! But before he went to the pictures he
singled Brill out.

"Have we found the missing man?" he asked, and
then the name came to him. "Alan Holmes, wasn't it?"

Brill looked absolutely exhausted, much more so than
a heavy day should warrant; he had the appearance of a
man suffering under great strain.

"Alan Holmes, sir. No, I'm afraid not."

"Is the search finished?"

"Just about an hour ago, sir."

"I couldn't be more sorry," Gideon said. "Is there anything we can do?"

"I don't think so, sir," Brill answered. "His wife's got
her mother with her and she's as well as she can be in the
circumstances. She thinks the same as the rest of us—that
he may have been dumped into the water."

This was one of the worst possible situations, Gideon
knew; tragedy for the wife and family, failure for the
police, and a hovering uncertainty for both. Before he
could speak again, Lemaitre came hurrying in, wearing a
trilby hat on his big, turnip-shaped head, and his pepper-
and-salt suit and polka-dot bow tie.

Lemaitre bore down on Gideon as Hobbs and Upway came up, Hobbs saying, "He's been to see the magistrate."

"All fixed up; he'll sit into the small hours if need be," Lemaitre said, and gripped Gideon's hand with his cold and bony fingers. "Now all we've got to do is sort the baskets out, isn't it?" He looked at Hobbs and Upway, and then all of them moved toward the photographs. Characteristically, Lemaitre went on as if he were the only one with anything worthwhile to say. "George— Commander, one of the Fleet Street chaps thinks some of these baskets are ex-Fascists—if 'ex' is right—who volunteered for the Biafra and Congo mercenaries. He was there, taking photographs. And if they are, they don't work for nothing any more. They attacked today like trained guerrillas; the only mistake they made was not being prepared for organized opposition. The point is, if they're being paid, who's paying them?"

"And another point," put in Hobbs, "is that if this was a professionally planned raid, then it's even more serious than if the motive was solely political. Do *you* recognize any of them?"

Gideon went closer. The photographs, all blown up, showed excellent likenesses. One, with a long, low shed in the background, showed three men with scaling ladders climbing over the dock walls, obviously preparing to take the dockers from the rear. Drawing still closer, feeling that some of the faces were familiar, he was now fully aware that he had been brought here because he could give a quick decision on whether the suspect men should be put up at tonight's special court, and—almost certainly —released with suspended sentences, or whether they should be held all night and inquiries made before tomorrow's hearing. He had no doubt that they should be held, and was on the point of saying so when Malcolm Brill, who had been looking at the photo with the shed in the background, gave a choking cry.

"*Willis!*" he shouted. "Did anyone search that old packing shed for Old Homer?"

The shed was so close to the gate that it could have been overlooked, or left by everyone to others, Willis Murdoch admitted. Suddenly there was both hope and dread among all who were present.

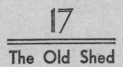

17

The Old Shed

THE CRY from Brill came at 6:41 precisely.

The message from a police radio car standing outside the cinema went out at 6:42 and was received by a police car standing close by the Number 1 Gate simultaneously. The police officer in charge put his head out the car window and shouted above the traffic noises to a P.L.A. man on duty at the gates.

"Search that old packing shed for Old Homer!"

Two dockers, coming out after a day's work which included the glorious free fight, a search, and overtime, turned and ran back, and the police car moved toward the gates. The P.L.A. policeman called out to other dockers coming away from the wharves; in the distance a ship's siren roared. Men passed on the order, and the first to reach the shed was a burly Irishman wearing hobnailed boots. He took a running jump at the rickety door and planted a foot against the rotting panels halfway up. The panels broke, the door sagged. Men and light streamed onto the rotting racks on one side, the rubbish, the filth in the place. One man went flying as he kicked a piece of metal which clanged and echoed. A smaller docker pushed past the Irishman—and then stopped, shouting, *"He's here!"*

Every man near the shed stopped, as if switched off. But it was only a few seconds before they began to move, and at 6:46 the mummified-looking body of Old Homer was lifted off a heap of broken packing cases and carried by two men toward the open air. Inside and outside the shed, the same things were being said, the same questions asked.

"They found Old Homer!"

"Is he dead?"

"Looks like a goner, mate."

"They've stuck his bloody mouth up."

"Looks like murder to me."

"Old Homer . . . dead . . . murder . . . Make way, there. Here's the first aid."

Almost before they had dabbed the sticking plaster with alcohol and pulled it off, very gently, an ambulance bell sounded. The ambulance men hurried with a stretcher as the sleeping bag and the strips of canvas were cut from Alan Holmes. He was limp, still, lifeless. The rumor that he was dead grew stronger, and it flashed around the docks and the dock area. Before seven o'clock, it was already being talked about in The Docker and the other pubs nearby.

Malcolm Brill heard it when he was with the police at the Regality Cinema, after Gideon had gone and when the unidentified men, none of whom gave a name or made a comment when charged, had been moved to Brixton Prison, the only place where there were cells enough to hold them all for the night. To Brill, the routine of the charge had become almost ludicrous.

Whoever made the charge would say, "I am a police officer and it is my duty to charge you with committing a breach of the peace; to wit . . . It is also my duty to inform you that you have the right to remain silent but that anything you say may be written down and used as evidence in court."

Brill was torn three ways, all savagely.

He wanted to see this affair through but was desperately anxious to find out Old Homer's condition; he wanted to help Harriet Holmes; and he wanted to know what was happening at his own home. The scene he had looked down on the previous night had been etched so deeply onto his mind that it was as if it had been branded on with red-hot irons.

A C.I.D. man came in from the street, briskly. The foyer was now nearly empty: Hobbs had gone, Lemaitre and some of his officers were dealing with the charges in what had once been the manager's office; a few newspapermen still stood about.

The C.I.D. man said to a colleague, "That poor devil Holmes has had it."

"Dead?" asked the colleague.

"Yep."

"Tough luck," the colleague replied.

Tough luck, Brill thought savagely. Tough luck, tough luck! He turned and hurried out to his hired car. *Tough luck, tough luck.* God! This would tear Harriet Holmes into raw and bleeding pieces. *Tough luck, tough luck.* He drove toward the Dockside Hospital, where they had taken Old Homer, and saw another newspaperman in the small bare entrance hall, with its finger signs to various wards and departments.

"Do you know where Holmes is?"

"Accident emergency ward—along there." The man pointed.

Brill hurried along a narrow passage, ignoring a porter who called, "Where do you think you're going?" He saw a sign saying, "ACCIDENT WARD," and turned in to another passage. The astringent smell of antiseptics was very sharp. Two nurses came along, one white, one black, both giggling. He saw another sign on a door: "WAITING ROOM." *Tough luck, tough luck, tough luck.* He opened the door and saw Harriet Holmes, holding the hands of an older woman, tears streaming down her plump cheeks, but certainly not tears of grief. She was half crying, half shouting.

"Thank God; oh, thank God; oh, thank God!" Then she turned her head and saw Brill. Her eyes became radiant; she dropped the older woman's hands and sprang toward him. Suddenly they were hugging each other like lovers who had been parted for an age. "He's all right," she said, sobbing. "He's alive, he'll be all right. Oh, thank God!"

Soon, Brill was able to leave her, more quiet of heart and mind than he had been for many hours. He had nothing more to do at the Regality Cinema or at the docks. The obvious thing was to go home.

He could not remember a time when he felt, as he did now, that he did not want to see Rose. He sat for a few minutes, at the wheel of his car, looking at the hospital on one side and the dock on the other. Cranes were clanking, a shift of dockers was going into the main gate, everything was normal. Suddenly, he started the engine and moved off. It was no use postponing the evil day, but what would he feel like when he saw her?

He remembered how he had felt like murder last night.

This morning he had got out of bed while she had been fast asleep, and had left a note saying, "I've an early assignment." Even then he had hardly been able to think clearly; had they argued, had there been the slightest excuse, he might well have become violent. He could surely control himself now. He wondered if he ought to have a drink, and decided not to. He felt tired out, but the relief at hearing that Old Homer would recover remained a calming factor. And he had seen the police at work, particularly Gideon and Hobbs, in a way he had never seen before. Gideon could not have given orders for that shed to be searched more quickly had they been looking for his own son.

Brill drove across the Tower Bridge, pulling in for a moment and looking down into the Pool of London. This helped to calm him further, with its sense of history and of man's own impermanence. He went the long way round to his home and it was half past eight when he pulled up a few doors away from his house, passing the window where Dorothy had been watching, excited at sight of him. She would be in bed now, and so would her brother

Roger. He got out of the car as a door farther along the street opened and a young woman whom he knew slightly, a friend of Rose's more than of his, came hurrying.

"Malcolm!" There was urgency in her voice.

"Yes?" His heart contracted.

"Malcolm, Dorothy's been taken ill; they think it's poisoning. Rose is half demented. Roger's with me."

Brill caught his breath. "Where—"

"They're at home—there's a doctor with Dorothy now."

Brill turned, ran the few yards to his own front door, jumped up the steps, key in hand. As he opened the door, he grabbed to prevent it from banging. He heard a voice upstairs. He went up, very quickly, and saw Rose coming out of the bathroom, carrying an enamel bowl.

She stood stock-still, and cried, "Oh, thank God you're here."

"How is she?" Brill demanded.

"The doctor's used a stomach pump. We should know soon."

He took the bowl from her and put an arm around her waist as they went into the child's bedroom. A young Pakistani doctor stood at the side of Dorothy's bed and a Jamaican nurse was wiping the child's face with a damp sponge. Dorothy lay on her back, her eyes closed, breathing heavily. The doctor looked up at Brill, and as he spoke his teeth were very white against his skin.

"I have good reason to hope she will recover. You are the father?"

"Yes."

"I have done all I can do now, I assure you." The man spoke with great deliberation. "I will call again later in the evening. The nurse will stay for a little while so your wife can get some rest." He turned to Rose. "Do not worry, Mrs. Brill. She is a very strong child. You have taken the best care of her. I am sure her powers of recovery will be very great. Now excuse me, please. I have more patients to see."

He moved toward and past them.

The nurse began to collect the equipment that had been in use: the stomach pump with its long tube, the surgical bowls, the cotton wool, the antiseptics. In a deeper, richer voice than the man's, she said, "I'm sure you don't have anything to worry about now. I can manage up here very well, if you would like to get your husband something to eat, Mrs. Brill." She almost shooed them away, and they went out and down the stairs.

They were in the small, modernized kitchen when suddenly Rose turned and huddled against Malcolm and began to cry. He soothed her. He caressed her. The tears streamed and her shoulders and her whole body shook; exhausted though he was, he forgot everything but her distress.

Soon she began to calm down.

At last, she drew away, sniffling, and when he gave her his handkerchief she blew into it heavily and then dabbed at her eyes. It was a long, long time since he had seen Rose looking so plain. The picture gradually superseded the one which had been in his mind all day.

Slowly, they returned to a semblance of normal, and she took something out of the oven.

"A sausage toad," she said. "It will be done to death."

In fact the batter in which the sausages had been baked looked dried up, but he could not have cared less. She also took out the remains of a creamy-looking rice pudding; she made milk dishes extremely well. As he began to eat the sausage toad she put coffee on in a percolator and placed two cans of beer on the table.

She was opening one, and he was eating with a surprisingly good appetite, when out of the blue she said, "Don't let me go out without you again. Don't *ever,* do you understand? If you can't come, I'll stay at home. If I hadn't been out last night, this might never have happened. The family must come first, *make* me understand that!"

He thought, God give me the sense never to tell her what I saw.

It was a strange feeling: a combination of hurt and jealousy, of pain and pleasure, of gladness and sadness.

He said, "I think you do understand it, darling."

She turned her back on him and went to the larder. She was there for so long that he felt sure she was crying, but soon she came back with a freshly opened pot of the gooseberry jam she had made the previous summer. She poured coffee, and said, "I'll take a cup up to the nurse. She's been wonderful, I don't care what they say about colored people." She pushed a cup toward Brill and then hurried out of the little kitchen.

18

Policy and Politics

LORD SIMON NAGEL picked up a decanter from the damask-covered dining table in the long, narrow, beautifully paneled room, and asked, "Brandy with your coffee, Commander?" His voice was rather high pitched, a characteristic of the Nagels for generations. So were his hooked nose, his fleshy jowl, his long upper lip. He was a big man but not so massive as Gideon, with iron-gray hair. The portraits of the seven earls who had preceded the present one looked down at them, one hung on each panel, and at either end was a picture of a woman: the wife of the first earl, and the wife of the present one. This had become a tradition and the Nagels were great traditionalists.

Gideon said, "May I have brandy later?"

"By all means. Or would you prefer port?"

Gideon thought, I wish he wouldn't fuss so much; and then he came to a startling conclusion: that Nagel was nervous. They had talked about the immigration situation over a homely dinner of roast beef and Yorkshire pudding, with delicately cooked vegetables, apple pie with cream, and one of the most flavorful Stiltons Gideon had tasted for years. He would never want a better meal.

"Brandy for me," he said.

"Charles?" Nagel and Mesurier, it proved, were old friends.

"Brandy," Mesurier said.

"I think we'll take the big chairs," decided Nagel; there were three huge armchairs along one end of the room, and he proffered them and cigars, then placed a trolley with port and brandy and glasses, as well as some plain chocolate mints, so that all could reach, before going on: "Commander, what exactly would you like me to do?"

Gideon, although expecting the question, was nevertheless not ready for it.

"To say exactly isn't easy," he hedged.

"No. I understand that. However—you have stated in clearest terms a very grave social problem. It has become obvious that this greatly concerns you, distresses you, and you feel—forgive me if I am wrong—you feel that the situation is both more than the police can properly control and more than they should be expected to. And you state that you have an uneasy feeling that you only scratch the surface of the problem, that much more is going on than any of us realize."

"Or can find out," Mesurier said.

"That's about right," Gideon admitted, warming to the subject. "I think public opinion needs to be aroused, so the public need informing as a first move."

"But how can they be informed if the full facts are not known?" countered Nagel.

"That's what we must find out," Gideon said. "The full facts, I mean."

"But as you've said, only the Home Office, being in control of home affairs, and the local authorities can do that," Nagel reminded him. "You want me—or some newspaper—to take the issue up so that the government and the local authorities are vitually compelled to make greater efforts."

"Exactly," Gideon approved heartily.

"You must see the one almost insuperable difficulty," Nagel said.

"I see difficulties, but not insuperable ones," retorted Gideon.

"Then I doubt if you see the one that worries me." Nagel poured out port for himself and the light glinted on it, ruby red. "If any newspaper takes this up as an issue, then it will be accused of political motivation. You *can* see that, can't you?"

"Does it matter, provided there is no political motivation?" asked Gideon.

Nagel sipped, paused, sipped again, and said, "Yes, Commander, it does. A case against a newspaper doesn't have to be proved, as in court. It is simply rumor or word of mouth. If the *Daily Star* took this case up as the situation stands at present, then all of the Unity Press group would be accused of having a political angle. Since our politics *are* right-inclined, we would be strongly accused of trying to create a situation which would make it more difficult for a left-wing government to control the problem of both immigration and integration. And we would doubtless be accused of undermining any right-wing government."

Gideon said heavily, "I see."

He should have expected this, of course; he should not have felt so hopeful, so optimistic, simply because several things had gone right. He should have known that Nagel, like any newspaper owner, would first have to consider the economics of his newspapers, and take every action with distribution in mind. He could not simply take sides for an ideal, for a cause. He had to justify whatever he did in terms of circulation and advertising revenue.

"But the *Daily Star* is wholly independent," Mesurier said. "It doesn't have to care what is said about it."

Nagel looked at him from beneath his lashes, broodingly.

"I wouldn't say that, Charles. No newspaper can be wholly independent from its advertisers, for instance."

"I thought that was what you were saying, in spite of your inclination to the right," remarked Mesurier.

"No," contradicted Nagel. "I was stating the facts as I see them. Commander, you know, don't you, that no newspaper can change government policies, and even though one tries it can seldom influence government attitudes." The question was rhetorical and Gideon knew there was no need to answer. "However, the public can change policies on occasions. Do I understand you to mean that you believe that the situation in Britain concerning the conditions of life for many colored immigrants is so bad that if the people knew how bad, they would demand action to improve it?"

Gideon said, heart rising, "That is exactly what I believe."

"Simon—" Mesurier began.

"Let me think a minute, Charles." Nagel silenced the other with a glance as well as the words and leaned back. There was no sound at all in the room except the breathing of the three men, until he sat up, sipped the port, and went on almost as if he were addressing a public meeting. "Are you also implying that neither the Home Office nor the local authorities want to probe too deeply for fear of what they'll find out if they do?"

Gideon nodded, but before he could speak Mesurier said, "Whether Gideon thinks that or not, I think it."

"Some local authorities are much better than others," Gideon remarked.

"No doubt." Nagel spoke as if he were really thinking about something else. "Commander—" He paused.

"Yes, sir?"

"Commander, by 'political' I don't necessarily mean party political, of course. I mean that the newspaper would be accused of forcing this issue because it believed that the nation was in danger. And most people, especially those who would oppose us or revile us, would assume that by danger we meant social danger; that we were concerned with keeping Britain white, and were opposed to mixed marriages and integration and indeed most immigration. It would be said that although over many years we have argued that a human being is a human being and the color of his skin should not be held either for or against him, we are in fact rigidly anti-Communist and think a man's political opinions should be held against him if they can be considered treasonable. It *will* be said, I must emphasize, that in truth we are opposed to colored immigration. There are aspects of the immigration situation which I don't like, but I am not and the policy of my newspapers is not anti-color. However, it could be made to appear so if we went to take up this cause, and I don't want that to happen."

He sat back in his chair again and sipped port, giving the impression that he had said all that needed saying. Mesurier stirred but did not speak. Gideon's mind was working very fast, as it always did when a problem on which he had concentrated for a long time was brought to a head. He had a sense of great tension; a feeling that Nagel was looking for but hadn't yet found a way of helping without taking the risks which were undoubtedly there.

Suddenly, Mesurier asked, "What circulation would you drop, Simon?"

"Probably twenty-five thousand—what's left of what we absorbed when we took over the *Clarion*. Too much," he added. "We would not hold all our advertisers, and you don't need telling how significant they are."

Mesurier said, "I know only too well," and shifted again in his chair.

Gideon was very still, aware of the gaze of the other two men. It was almost as if they were expecting a miracle from him. And at the back of his mind there was something which he couldn't quite bring to the surface.

To fill in what could become an awkward pause, or else to justify himself for his caution, Nagel went on, "Commander, I don't have to tell you that the economics of Fleet Street are as difficult and in some ways as shaky as the nation's. Most newspapers are working on a very slender margin. A few can ride out almost any crisis, but others can't—that is why so many have died in the past twenty years. The *Daily News* has a readership peculiarly its own and is likely to hold it provided it maintains its political and social attitudes. The *Star*, however, is the smallest of the mass-circulation newspapers, and is the target of all the fierce competition of the truly big ones. We are in constant danger of being squeezed out. One false move and we would go." Nagel glanced across at Mesurier, as if pleading for collaboration although he did not ask for it.

Mesurier volunteered: "It won't help Gideon if you say no although you wish you could say yes, but—for what it's worth, the Fleet Street strike was postponed because the owners were able to offer incontrovertible figures showing that a two-week strike would put the *Daily News* out of business, and four weeks would finish the *Daily Star*. Until the last minute, no one believed us."

Nagel asked, "How about that brandy?"

"No," Gideon said, almost sharply. "No. Do I understand you would do what you can if you felt it safe for the newspaper?"

"Yes," Nagel answered.

"And being safe from the charge of political motivation would be sufficient?"

"Yes," Nagel answered, as quickly and as positively.

"So if there were a proven danger to the country, not simply political danger in the sense that you've talked about today, you could proceed?"

Now both men watched him without moving, as if they were suddenly hypnotized. And in a way he felt as if *he* were hypnotized, by an idea. He was caught again with his problem of finding exactly the right words to say what he meant. The sense of tremendous importance of his mission increased, as if this could go one way and end in disaster, or go the other way and be a success beyond his wildest hopes. He must find the right words, *must* say exactly what he meant, not grope as he had with Nigel Simply.

Suddenly, he demanded, "If you had reason to believe that what happened at the docks today was part of a nationwide attempt to change the government's policies by force, would *that* be the answer?"

Mesurier said, as if to himself, "Well, well, well!"

"Go on," urged Nagel.

"These so-called Strike Breakers consisted mainly of trained mercenaries, men with guerrilla warfare training and experience. They thought it would be a cakewalk today; that's why they ran into trouble. They came to frighten the dockers out of striking. Their real strike-breaking weapon was fear. At least twenty-five of them will be up for first hearing tomorrow. We shall ask for eight days' remand in custody to make inquiries. I think we shall prove beyond doubt what they were up to—civil interference by violence. Would *that* be a strong enough motive to justify you taking a stand?"

Very quietly but with shared tension, Nagel asked, "Can it be applied to the immigration problem?"

"This afternoon we found a cellar in East London packed full of Pakistani 'immigrants'," Gideon said. "They had come ashore last night near Shoreham in Sussex and were traced to London. Just before we raided the houses where they were being hidden, a man attempted to throw two phosgene canisters into a special ventilation shaft. Had the canisters gone down into the cellars, all of the men would have suffered, most would have died. It is virtually certain—certain enough for you to base an argument on it—that this was a cold-blooded attempt to kill the Pakistanis. And," went on Gideon, in a voice which vibrated throughout that paneled room, "photographs taken at the docks show the man who tried to kill the Pakistanis was in that raid, but obviously he escaped. Is that enough? One was an attempt to break a strike by force. The other was an attempt to murder unlawful immigrants. Both are examples of using violence as a political weapon. *Is* that enough?"

When he had finished, Gideon felt himself sweating—at the neck and forehead, in the small of his back, and under his chin. His mouth was parched, too, but for the moments that followed he could do no more than sit back, looking at Nagel, glancing at Mesurier, and aware that the smaller man was also tense and strained. Then Gideon gulped, and he sipped what was left of his cold coffee.

The movement was the signal for Nagel to move in his chair also, and for him to say, "Yes."

The single word was everything Gideon wanted to hear, and yet at first its full force did not dawn on him. "Yes." Gradually, understanding came: yes, it *was* enough for Nagel to take up the cause. Could the man mean it? Could he have misunderstood? Nagel was now sitting forward, gripping both arms of his chair, and Mesurier was leaning back at full length, his long pale hands over his face.

Nagel repeated, "Yes, Commander. We shall link these two events together on our front page in the morning. We shall run a leading article which will insist that the danger in the industrial front and over immigrants is so great that the full facts must be discovered and divulged. *Yes,*" he repeated, standing up and looking at the portrait of the old woman at their end of the room. She was so lined and yet she looked so alive and alert and wise.

For the first time, Gideon saw the words on a small plaque on the bottom of the frame. They read: "If the cause is just—dare all."

He had no shadow of doubt that the motto was coursing through Nagel's mind.

It was Mesurier who spoke next, very quietly, as if he were exhausted and having difficulty in speaking. Gideon reminded himself that it was less than two days since he had talked to this man about the subject; and only now did he realize what a strain Mesurier had been living under.

"Will it be better if I take the same theme, do you think? Or support you the next day?"

"Support me," Nagel said. "Don't give anyone a chance

to say we got into a huddle to turn this into a circulation booster. Commander, I shall need to send two or three of the *Star*'s best men to see you or anyone you care to nominate, so that we get all the facts and figures right. I imagine you would prefer someone else."

"Three people," Gideon said quietly. "My deputy, Alec Hobbs, who has been in direct charge of the dock situation. Superintendent Lemaitre of NE Division, who was present when the attempt to murder the men in the cellar was made. And—you'll need to do this by telephone, I'm afraid—Superintendent Honiwell, who has been working on the problem of illegal immigration for months. He's up in Lowestoft, and you'll probably need to go through the local Superintendent, named—" He broke off, frowning. The name was on the tip of his tongue but he could not think of it. But Hobbs would, and if the worst came to the worst, the *Daily Star* would have to go direct to Honiwell. Suddenly he realized that he hadn't begun to tell Nagel how much he thought of the decision.

"Commander," Nagel said, "you've given me a chance to take positive action. I've wanted for a long time to commit myself to a cause." He stood smiling at Gideon, and suddenly turned to Mesurier and said, "Are you satisfied, Charles?"

"I'll be satisfied when we've really got the government moving," Mesurier said. "But I think this will do the trick. I really think it will. Now! I must get back to my office. Can I give you a lift, Commander?"

"I've a car," Gideon said, and went on quickly, "If I could use the telephone—"

He talked to Hobbs on one line as Nagel was talking to his news editor on another, and Hobbs promised to alert both Honiwell and Lemaitre. There was excitement in his voice as he responded. Gideon knew that this mattered at least as much to Hobbs as it did to him.

Word went from Nagel to the news editor, from the news editor to the composing and the machining rooms.

Hold the front page of the *Daily Star*. Word went out from the managers to the foremen. Everything else could be run, but not page 1 and so not pages 2 and 15 and 16. Soon men in the big rooms by the side of the huge machines were standing idle. A few complained, most slipped away for a cup of tea or a cigarette. Rumors started. The huge rolls of paper stood idle, both on and off the Heidelburgs. The smell of printers' ink, of lead, of newsprint seemed to get stronger as the time dragged on. Outside, men began to fret as they waited by vans to rush the earlier editions to the stations to catch the last trains to the provinces; unless a move came through, some trains would be missed. Messages flashed to and fro, but the front page did not come. Gradually, the presses stopped rolling, all the work they could do finished.

Out in the field, the *Star's* top newsmen questioned, pleaded, argued, gradually created part of the story. First, Hobbs's. Next, Lemaitre's. At last, Honiwell's. As the stories were sent in by teletype and telephone, the men in the subeditors' room began to work at speed. Gainswell, the best news editor on Fleet Street, read the stories, read the galley proofs as they were pulled. Three men and a girl sat with him, cutting, comparing stories with photographs, putting in subheadings. Gradually, he pasted up the front page, selected the photographs, ordered the type size for headlines and subheadlines. When the page looked ready to go, he snatched it up and ripped it across and across. A little man, bald but for a fringe of black hair, snipped off more of the headlines, bunched them, ran them in the shape of a diamond in the center of the page.

Someone gasped, "My God!"

Gainswell didn't speak but breathed through his wide-open mouth, picked up a big pencil, and filled in the diamond. Across the middle were the words:

BRITAIN IN DANGER.

Above, he scribbled:

DOCKS
BATTLE

and below he scrawled:

IMMIGRANT
SHIPLOADS
DIE

Then he used his pencil at incredible speed, showing where the stories already set and proofed should go. Now his assistants worked with him; before long there was a paste-up as simple as could be to follow. Across the top of the page beneath the title, photographs—of Gideon, Hobbs, Willis Murdoch, a Pakistani, Old Homer, Lemaitre, another Pakistani, a ship. Across the foot, more photographs—of the prisoners, Harriet Holmes, a Pakistani girl, a helmeted policeman. Soon a full paste-up was spread over his desk.

He stood back and examined it—and then he said, "Let's go."

The page was rushed downstairs, the molds were made, the presses started, the great rollers turned; the folded newspapers came out, were counted automatically, were bundled and pushed onto a conveyor, and were carried up to the waiting vans. Men worked as if their lives depended on it, stacks were wrapped and labeled, engines roared, and fumes stank, and the vans went out to feed the multitudes who would expect the papers in the morning.

They went to the heart of London.

They went to the heart of each big city.

They went to the country towns, the villages, the hamlets.

They went into letter boxes and into racks.

And one of them was tucked into Gideon's letter box

before he woke, while another was pushed through the letter box of a house in Highgate owned by John Winfrith.

Gideon, when he saw that front page, felt exhilarated to a point of exultation. He read every word of every story, the quotes from man after man, fully convinced that the dangers in the situation had been vividly portrayed so that no reader could be in doubt. The people would listen and, my God, the authorities would listen, too! He would never again feel that the police were fighting this battle on their own.

John Winfrith stared at the headlines and the stories and the photographs. There were so many evidences of his failure. The fact that all the dockers arrested at the docks had been bound over to keep the peace, which really meant allowed to escape scot-free, was one of the worst.

Nine out of ten of his men languished in Brixton jail and, he felt sure, would be remanded in custody for at least a week. All the hatred he felt for the society and the people he believed to be ruining it welled up in him; and one face peered up at him—the face of the one man whom he blamed above all others.

19

The Big Machines

GIDEON, WHO DROVE HIMSELF to the Yard that morning, pulled up outside the newspaper shop in the New Kings Road, and as he stepped toward the doorway, he saw that all the newspapers were jammed into the racks outside. Several customers were inside and Gideon hesitated for a moment before going in; he was eager to glance at the front pages but not to be kept waiting. The gray-haired, garrulous man behind the counter caught sight of him and waved a *Daily Star* above his head.

"You seen this, Mr. Gideon?"

"Gideon," a man echoed.

"Mr. Gideon," a second exclaimed, and the couple who had just left also turned and stared.

Willy-nilly, Gideon went in, welcomed by the news agent with a broad smile, rare in one usually overearnest. He handed Gideon the *Star* and said, "You can have that with my compliments, sir. Wonderful job at the docks, that was, and—have you seen the *Examiner?*"

"No," Gideon said.

"*That's* with my compliments, too," said the news agent. "Page 3, Mr. Gideon—and you've proper hogged the whole of 'Simply' this morning!"

Gideon opened the copy of the *Examiner,* rather like the *Daily Telegraph* in appearance, and there he was, looking out from the columns, not a big photograph but one extremely well printed; obviously a special block had been made. Slightly self-conscious because so many pairs of eyes were concentrated on him, he skimmed the column—in fact, over two and a half columns of the top half of the page with the heading "Simply Speaking." He had no idea what to expect, although the news agent would hardly have drawn attention to the piece had it been unfriendly.

Simply had written:

If Commander George Gideon, O.B.E., really had his way, the lot of the policeman, from the London and (he is careful to make clear) the provincial bobby up to the senior ranks of the hierarchy of Scotland Yard, would be a much happier one. And lighter. . . and more successful . . . and much worse for the bad man: the criminal.

For the Commander, powerful in body, voice, and opinions, says simply that society is responsible for too much crime. . . . That the police too often have to clean up the situation created by the mistaken policies of some politicians, past and present, in local government and in Westminster.

The Commander is, of course, fully aware that there may be some in high office who do not think he should express these views, no matter how strongly he may hold them. However, he has had some thirty years in the Metropolitan Police Force. He literally worked himself up from the beat. He holds one of its highest ranks with great distinction. Some of Scotland Yard's greatest triumphs are directly attributable to him, although he prefers to talk of team effort. He was the prime mover in the dramatic coup at London's docks yesterday when the bloodiest riots in British history were avoided by a fraction of time and the courage and efficiency of the police.

He says the answer to our rising crime rate is not simply more police but fewer causes of crime. In a society in which nearly everything goes, the crime rate is bound to soar because the incentives are so great.

I rate this, very simply, as common sense from the Commander. It is widely known that the Home Office—like all Ministries—frowns upon statements of opinion from its servants, and for some reason I find difficult to understand, the Home Office appears to regard the police as its servants rather than the public's.

The police *are* public servants, doing an extremely difficult job in a thorough, painstaking, efficient way occasionally shot with brilliance. I have a piece of advice for the Home Office.

Don't reproach Commander George Gideon, O.B.E., for his outspoken manner. Persuade him, if he can be persuaded, to be the chief public relations officer for the police of the land. In fact, an ombudsman. This would be yet another glowing triumph for common sense.

Gideon, still aware of the gaze of at least half a dozen people, folded the newspaper and said, a little gruffly, "Very flattering." He wasn't sure how he felt. A little heavy-hearted, perhaps, or apprehensive: in one way Simply had gone further than he had expected. But if it were possible to remove his, Gideon's, name from the column, there would be nothing at all with which he would disagree; it was exactly what he believed to be true. These things were going through his mind as he picked up one of the morning's newspapers, insisted on paying for all but the *Examiner,* and made his way out of the shop to the wide pavement.

There he was astounded!

At least fifty people had gathered, many of them waving newspapers. Most were men, but women and some teen-age girls were among them, as well as three boys with hair down to their shoulders and clothes adorned with sewn-on badges, pieces of velvet and ribbon, peace badges, and buttons. A dozen copies of the *Star* were turned, face toward him, with that remarkable diamond effect in the middle. On the fringe of the crowd were three policemen, one of them the man who had come to tell him he was wanted by the City Police—good Lord, little more than forty-eight hours ago! There was spontaneous cheering as Gideon appeared, and startled though he was, he could not keep back a smile of sheer pleasure. A man called, "Good old Gee-Gee!" and others took up the nickname. He waved as he bore down toward his car, where the familiar policeman opened a door.

"Good morning, sir!"

"Good morning," said Gideon. "Is anyone after me this morning?"

The man's responding grin was as broad as Gideon's.

"Looks as if everybody is, sir!"

Gideon laughed as he got in and took the wheel. There was another, louder cheer as he started off, with traffic behind him held up by one of the policemen. He slid out into the empty familiar road, passing the open space of the Eelbrook Common, where the late office workers were still hurrying across the green toward Fulham Broadway, which he had known for so long as Walham Green. So much changed, yet so much was exactly the same. Soon he was reflecting less generally. Either the *Star*'s front page or the "Simply Speaking" column would have been enough for one morning; the two together were almost too much.

It was already half past nine, later than he liked to arrive, although hours as such had come to mean little to him. Traffic was stinking and thick as he neared Albert Bridge; nothing seemed to improve either the traffic or the fumes, and this Embankment drive could be so beautiful. It had been when he had first walked, later cycled, even when he had first driven along it. He was being very nostalgic this morning! Policemen on duty at the worst traffic spots singled him out for special treatment, and two or three on the pavement saluted him, but it was not until he reached Parliament Square and was saluted by four uniformed policemen in a row that he realized this was particular to the morning. If he had had a moment's doubt before, he could have had none when he reached the Yard, where man after man flicked a hand in salute or acknowledgment, from the uniformed men to a group of massive Flying Squad men and several senior detectives. *Two* hurried to open the car door for him.

"Good morning, sir." "Good morning." So it went on, up the steps, in the hall, toward his office.

Hobbs appeared from the cloakrooms, and as several men were about he was formal except for his broad smile. "Good morning, sir!"

"Good morning, Alec. If this goes on, I shall expect my office to be a bowerful of flowers."

Hobbs laughed, and opened the door for him. There, on his desk and on top of the filing cabinets, were three vases full of flowers! Hobbs began to chuckle, and after the first shock, Gideon laughed but was more touched than amused He went to a bowl of red roses, as nearly sure as he could be that they were from Kate. The card with them read, *"At last the reward you deserve. Love, Kate."* This was in her own handwriting, and Gideon raised his head to consider.

Hobbs told him, "She sent them up by a neighbor. They arrived half an hour ago."

"Humph," grunted Gideon. "Nice." He picked up a vase of mixed garden flowers, and the perfume was much stronger than that of the roses The card said, "Keep at it —Penny"; it was typewritten. "Very nice," he repeated.

"And don't get any false ideas," Hobbs said. "It was Penny's own idea; she telephoned me before I left my flat, and told me exactly what to buy and what to say."

"Bless her," Gideon said.

In that moment, the mood between them changed. In any case, it was a rare mood in the office, but so were the flowers and the brightness about them. Suddenly, however, Hobbs was a different man—younger, diffident.

Gideon, who had moved to pick up the third vase, little more than a posy, met the other man's gaze; he knew instinctively that Hobbs was going to talk about his relationship with Penny. So Gideon waited. He thought, Something is bound to go wrong; and he wondered if Hobbs, after all, had changed his mind. If he had, it would be a dreadful blow to Penny. She would try to hide it, of course, but it would hurt her. At least there would be the soundproofed attic. He did not know why, in those few seconds, he felt so sure that Hobbs was going to ask him to help him break the news: it was perhaps just the feeling that no morning could maintain such an upbeat swing.

"George," Hobbs said, "Penny's going up to Scotland this week has made me do a lot of thinking. I've waited for a long time, tried to make sure that she has had plenty of time and every opportunity of breaking with me if she wants to. But I think she's had time enough now. If she's agreeable, I'd like us to marry very soon—as soon as the banns can be called and arrangements made. Will it be too much of a wrench for Kate, do you think?"

So I was wrong, thought Gideon, with enormous relief. Thank God, I was wrong! He shook his head and said, "No. But too much time pressure could be a problem. Give them time to make proper preparations. Kate wouldn't forgive you if this weren't the whitest of weddings with all the accompaniments. Apart from that, I think we all feel you've lived on your own long enough, Alec. And Kate and I have lost any doubts we ever had."

"Thank you," Hobbs said gruffly.

Gideon, at a loss for words, simply waved his hands in disclaimer, and then picked up the posy. On a slip of paper, not a card, were two letters: "S.S.," without a single word. This was from Sabrina Sale, of course; and it was the first time she had come anywhere near revealing her feelings.

Then the interoffice telephone rang and Gideon picked up the receiver.

"Gideon," he said.

"Come and see me, Commander, will you?" asked the Commissioner. "Use the private door."

Sir Reginald Scott-Marle stood up from his desk: a tall, lean man in his middle fifties; iron-gray hair, regular features, a kind of aloofness of manner which made many people feel ill at ease, even many who had known him for years. The door leading to his secretary's room was closing as Gideon went in, so Scott-Marle had not been alone. Did that explain the use of "Commander"? Although Gideon had known this man for many years, liked and trusted him, and had a relationship which overlapped into friendship, he could still feel uncertain of himself. Now he wondered whether the "Simply Speaking" column had gone too far, whether Scott-Marle, who was in fact the man most in touch with the Home Office, felt he had said too much. Something had to go wrong!

Scott-Marle smiled at his friendliest, came around the desk, and gripped Gideon's forearm; and there was a note of laughter, of pleasure in his voice.

"Quite a morning for us, George—especially for you."

"I am waiting for the ground to cave in," Gideon countered.

"Nonsense! Nothing but good can possibly come out of this, and you will be intrigued to know that Sir Gordon Pettigrew telephoned me as soon as I got in this morning and asked if I had inspired the 'Simply Speaking' story and whether you might become available as a kind of liaison between all police forces in the country and the Home Office."

"Good God!"

"You really mean that surprises you?" asked Scott-Marle. "It doesn't surprise me at all, but that isn't why I asked you to come and see me. There's plenty of time for that later." So he was not going to raise the issue of the Assistant Commissionership. "As far as you yet know, is there a case against the men in custody for conspiracy?"

"Hobbs has been going through the records, where they are known," Gideon said. "He thinks there is a case. Lemaitre talked to him this morning by telephone, and the man who tried to put gas down the ventilation hole of the cellar has a badge in his pocket which is similar to badges held by over four hundred of the men under charge. It is a good-quality oak leaf and acorn made of brass. We've no record of it, and it obviously indicates membership of some organization. Lemaitre's prisoner hasn't talked, but one or two of the others have. All are viciously anti-color and anti-Communist. There doesn't seem any doubt at all that an organization exists. The problem is to find out how big it is—and how dangerous."

20

Sea and Air Search

MATTHEW HONIWELL woke in his bedroom at a small hotel on the sea front at Lowestoft and looked out onto the beach and the sunlit sea. Gulls were cawing. Several trawlers appeared to be at anchor, some distance off; a few rowboats were drawn up close to the promenade, some old men were mending nets. Only a few holiday-makers were about, mostly young men with children young enough to skip about with *joie de vivre* simply because they were at the seaside. A few puffs of white cloud showed toward the south. Two airplanes flew miles out to sea, and at least three motorboats were a mile or more offshore. Honiwell stretched, yawned, and then heard a tap at his door. This would be morning tea.

"Come in!" he called.

It was morning tea—brought in by fair-haired, blue-eyed Superintendent Cressy, who also carried the morning newspapers. Before Honiwell could recover from his shock, the other man slapped the tea tray down on the bedside table, and then spread the *Daily* Star over the bedclothes.

"Good God!" exclaimed Honiwell. He read avidly, drank tea, read more, and then demanded belatedly, "Was anything found here during the night?"

"No."

"Any more bodies?"

Cressy said, "Two, Matt."

"Are they searching again?"

"They've been at it since dawn," Cressy assured him.

Soon Honiwell was wallowing in sea that most people would have considered icy cold; then he hurried back to shave and shower, and took a last look out the window before going down to breakfast and to gloat over the newspapers. He felt, in common with every policeman in England, that this was a red-letter day for the police force throughout the land.

Honiwell, in that last look across the water of the North Sea, did not realize that he was looking in the direction of the S.S. *Breem,* which was drifting, helpless; and already dangerously near capsizing.

There were fifty-nine live men left in the hold.

Some were still strong enough to bang on the hatches and to shout, but no one came because there was no one to hear them.

Some were strong enough to keep their own heads above the thick, slimy water—half bilge, half sea water —coming in through a hole which was blocked by debris after an explosion in the engine room. A few tried to help others keep their heads up, so as to breathe. But every time the ship lurched with a wave the water in this hold went slowly, sluggishly over the heads of some, who gasped and spluttered and cried out in fear. Then, as the water receded, near quiet fell, but every mouth was closer to the level of the water.

The ship was settling.

It was not likely to remain afloat for another hour.

The new member of the crew of the fishing smack which had been close to the S.S. *Breem* for some time wore a badge on his jersey—an oak leaf with an acorn. From the quayside he scanned the horizon and the sky, seeing the searching craft in both sea and air. There was no talk among the men unloading their catches, nor among the men handing the baskets up and weighing them, of a ship going down or a ship being found.

When the catch was landed, he went to a telephone kiosk on the quay and called a London number. When a man answered, he said, "This is Calter. The job's done."

The man at the other end of the line, John Winfrith, said, "Come back to London as soon as you can, Calter. Do not show your badge."

"I'm not coming back to London, I'm through," Calter said. "I don't want to join the others in Brixton. Don't forget you owe me five hundred for this job."

"You'll get your money," Winfrith said coldly. "You would have got another thousand for the next job I had in mind. But I'll do that myself," he added, and repeated: "I'll do *that* one myself."

An R.A.F. helicopter from the Mildenhall Base, on loan to the police and stationed just off the coast south of Lowestoft, sighted the drifting ship almost the identical moment when Winfrith was putting down the receiver. The observer radioed their own and the drifting ship's approximate position, and reported: "We shall fly directly over the ship—stand by."

A minute later: "The ship is the S.S. *Breem,* registered at Hull."

And later: "There appears to be no one aboard; certainly no one is on deck or on the bridge. The ship is listing to port twenty-five to thirty degrees.. . . There is still no sign of life on board. . . . The hatches are battened down."

For a few moments there was silence, before Base replied, "Go as low as you can to check hatches. Other craft are on the way."

At that instant, helicopters, airplanes, motorboats, and torpedo boats all headed toward the S.S. *Breem.* The pilot took the helicopter so low that there seemed a danger of the landing bars striking the ship's rail, but the pilot lifted it clear, then turned in as small a circle as he could.

The observer, watching intently, saw what seemed to be a movement at one of the hatches, watched even more closely and saw the hatch move up a few inches and then drop down.

"Jim," he said to the pilot, "someone's in that hold."

"Don't be daft, Smithy."

"I tell you there is. Will you put me down?"

"If suicide is what you're after—" the pilot broke off and began to maneuver again over the unsteady ship. The observer dropped the rope ladder until it dangled on the deck, and then began to climb down. One moment his feet were almost touching the deck, the next they were three feet or more above, but at last he stepped off as casually as if this were a staircase in a house. Walking with care because the ship was rolling badly, he approached the hatch which had moved—and it moved again! One of the battens had become loose or the wedge had been carelessly fastened As he went to the other side, the observer saw a brown wrist straining against the hatch from underneath.

He looked up, pointed to the hatch, went unsteadily across, and then saw another wedge, also loose. Nearby was a marlinspike. He picked it up and prised at the wedge, not noticing other helicopters in the distance or the first of the motorboats in sight.

The wedge moved.

He shifted the batten from the hatch cover, then went down on his knees and tried to prise the cover up. He could hear water lapping inside. Now and again, he caught a glimpse of bright eyes in a dark face. Roaring above told of a second chopper hovering, and suddenly another man joined him and between them they heaved the hatch cover back. It crashed onto the deck as the observer and his companion stood for a moment, staring horrified at the heads and eyes above the water, eyes already closing to the brightness of the sun.

A motor torpedo boat drew alongside. . . .

"Fifty-seven men were rescued, seven were found

drowned or asphyxiated. The S.S. *Breem* foundered at 11:53 A.M." This teletype message, from Honiwell to Gideon and then from the Yard to the newspapers and to the news agencies, the radio and television stations, told the facts. The story in human fear and suffering was told partly in the local hospital, partly over the days and the weeks and the years which followed.

For Gideon, the news brought unrestrained relief. The sense that on this day something was bound to go wrong had been heavy within him even after he had come away from Scott-Marle's office. In his own office, working in the unaccustomed flower-perfumed air, he went through the papers prepared by Lemaitre and other divisional officers for the court hearings, all of which would be held after lunch. There was increasing evidence that these men were part of an organization which plotted the overthrow of law and order as he knew it. Some of the men were identified as extreme Fascists, who had left the unionist movement, saying that even its policies had become too mild for them. Several were known members of small, powerful guerrilla units which hired themselves out to the highest bidder. The fact that none would talk was itself a form of conspiracy; when so many men refused to volunteer statements, it was probable that they were under some kind of oath of secrecy.

There was no doubt at all, the police needed much more time to check.

There were now some four hundred men still being held in various police stations and the Brixton jail, and the hearings would be spread over three police courts. Lemaitre himself would make the main charges, and the deputy Public Prosecutor discussed the charge with Gideon and reached a simple conclusion. For the time being, it would be "conspiring with other individuals, known and unknown, to cause a breach of the peace." If all went smoothly, and there seemed no reason at all why it should not, the hearings should be over in less than an hour at each court.

Hobbs came in just after lunch—Hobbs, the policeman.

"Are you going to any of the courts yourself, George?"

"No," Gideon decided. "You do one, though. I expect Upway will go to another, and that will leave one for Lemaitre. I've had more than enough of the spotlight for the time being."

Hobbs gave a faint smile and said, "Once it starts, it often won't leave you alone. Have you given any thought to Simply's suggestion?"

Gideon leaned back in his chair, placed his hands on the arms, and looked very straight into Hobbs's eyes. He himself still did not want the post and Hobbs would, one day and before long, become the Assistant Commissioner for Crime. He, Gideon, could not expect always to be in his office as the Commander C.I.D. Changes were on the way, and could not be prevented or delayed for too long. There was just this one man at the Yard whom Gideon knew he could trust to be absolutely objective on the subject; who would have no axe to grind for himself or even for the police force and would consider only the interests of George Gideon.

So Gideon said quietly, "I've given some thought to it, Alec, and I'll give more. But before I do I'd like to know what you think."

"Given certain conditions, I think being a kind of ombudsman for the police could be exactly right," he said. "The day *is* coming when you will have to think of retiring, and I can't see you contentedly living at home, or traveling, or doing some kind of social work. Nor can I see you in any of the private security organizations, although they would give their right arms for you. Nor—"

The telephone rang, and he broke off. Gideon, nearer it, lifted the receiver, and a man said, "It's the Hall Sergeant here, sir. There's a gentleman to see you. He hasn't an appointment but he says he can give you some vital information about the Strike Breakers. If you know what I mean, sir."

"I know very well," Gideon said. "What is his name?"

"He's filled out the form, sir. He's a Mr. Winfrith—John Winfrith."

"Ask him to wait for a few minutes," Gideon said, and put down the receiver. "Do we know a John Winfrith?" he asked Hobbs, frowning. "There's the nuclear power station at Winfrith in Dorset—that may be why it sounds familiar. He claims to be able to give us vital information about the Strike Breakers."

"Supposing I go along and see if he seems reasonable or lunatic-fringe," Hobbs suggested.

Gideon hesitated, and then shook his head. He contemplated Hobbs for a few seconds before speaking in his quiet, measured voice.

"We'll talk about Simply and some other ideas when we've more leisure, Alec. There can't be any driving urgency, but you'll be amused to know that Pettigrew of the Home Office sounded the Commissioner this morning on the possibility that they might take Simply's suggestions seriously."

"Already!" exclaimed Hobbs.

"Before ten o'clock this morning."

"Then we don't need any more telling that the *Star's* front page and 'Simply Speaking' got home," said Hobbs, with deep satisfaction.

"We'll talk later," Gideon insisted, and put a hand on the telephone. "What was that chap's name? Inskip—no, Winfrith." He dialed the main hall. "Have Mr. Winfrith brought to my office," he ordered the man who answered. "This is Commander Gideon." He smiled up as Hobbs went out through the communicating door, then drew Kate's roses toward him. There were twelve, deep red roses of love. He touched the petals of one, then rather slowly a thorn. The one was velvet, the other like a steel claw. He had not seen Kate for nearly a week, and it was too long. Funny, Hobbs was feeling much the same about

Penny. How would that marriage work out? At least he had no shadow of doubt about Hobbs's eagerness, and he was quite certain that Penny wouldn't marry unless she both wanted to and felt ready.

There was a tap at the door from the passage.

"Come in," he called.

The door opened briskly; a sergeant came halfway in and said, "Mr. Winfrith, sir," and stood back as the silvery-haired stranger entered, a man whom Gideon thought at once looked very tense, with overbright, pale blue eyes. He looked to be in his early fifties, and his hair had a remarkable silvery sheen; his complexion was fair and blemish-free. He moved rather jerkily, but not toward Gideon: toward the middle of the room.

"Good morning," Gideon said. He was already wary, but only in case he had met a man who would prove to be a fanatic, a time-waster, the kind of man very difficult to get rid of. The perfume of Kate's roses wafted into his nostrils.

"Commander Gideon," Winfrith said. His voice was hard and distant.

"Yes, I am Commander Gideon."

"I have been wanting to meet you for a long time," said Winfrith, in that remote voice.

"That's very kind of you," Gideon said. "I understand you have some information about the organization called the Strike Breakers—vital information, I was told."

"I have indeed," affirmed Winfrith. "I am sure it is all the information you require, Commander Gideon. I know how many there are, what their duties are, where they live, how they make themselves known to each other, how they operate, their names and capabilities, even their records. I even know the name of their leader."

He stopped.

He drew an automatic pistol from the inside of his jacket, and smiled. His teeth were small and sharp-looking; the hand holding the gun was very steady.

"His name—my name—is Winfrith," he stated. "I have

come to kill you. At least I can make sure that you do nothing more to turn this once-proud nation into one of lazy layabouts and colored trash."

He raised the gun, and it covered Gideon's chest.

Gideon had no doubt at all that he was going to shoot; no doubt that he, George Gideon, was within an ace of death. He did not even have time to open his mouth and shout; he saw the tension at the man's forefinger, on the trigger, and he simply swept Kate's roses, vase and all, off the desk toward the man and at the same time threw himself to one side.

But he wasn't quick enough; by a fraction of a second, he wasn't quick enough.

The shot rang out, the bullet struck him in the left shoulder and sent him staggering. The man dodged to one side to get out of the way of the roses, and Hobbs's door opened; Hobbs had a chair in one hand, thrust forward as a shield. Gideon fell heavily to the floor. Winfrith leaped toward the passage door but it opened before he touched it. Two men flung themselves in, seeing but ignoring the gun. Winfrith fired twice, missing each time, before the men closed on him and brought him down.

Hobbs was on one knee, beside Gideon, whose forehead was bleeding and who lay absolutely still.

"Kate," Hobbs said into the telephone, "he's all right, I promise you. He caught his forehead on a corner of the desk and that knocked him out. He *was* shot, but high up near the shoulder in the fleshy part of the chest. I doubt if a bone is even cracked. He's on his way to Charing Cross Hospital, and when I saw him last he was taking an intelligent interest in everything going on about him, as well as telling everybody what to do.

"He's all right, Kate.

"Whatever the newspapers or the radio might say, he's all right. In fact, if you play your cards well you might even persuade him to take a month's holiday; he could accept it better if it were called convalescence.

"Just don't worry, there's really no need.

"Even if he had been killed, what he's done would have been well worth dying for," Hobbs declared, in a very firm voice. "But he's not been killed, and he'll live for years to help see this thing through."

There is nothing like spending an evening with a good Popular Library

Mystery